JOHN CONNOR was born on 4 November 1947 in Blackburn, Lancashire. He was brought up in children's homes in the North of England and emigrated to Australia in 1965 where he eventually trained and worked as a nurse. Since arriving in New Zealand in 1982 he has been a tutor in the Health Studies Department of Manukau Polytechnic. He received honourable mentions in numerous short story competitions and in 1987 won the Western Districts Writers competition with his story 'Man of Fire'. In 1989 he was co-winner of the inaugural Heinemann Reed Fiction Award. He is married and lives in Kingsland, Auckland.

DISTORTIONS

JOHN CONNOR

PACIFIC WRITERS SERIES

Published by Reed Books,
a division of Octopus Publishing Group (NZ) Ltd,
39 Rawene Road, Birkenhead, Auckland.
Associated companies, branches and representatives
throughout the world.

This book is copyright. Except for the purpose of fair
reviewing, no part of this publication may be reproduced
or transmitted in any form or by any means, electronic or
mechanical, including photocopying, recording, or any
information storage and retrieval system, without
permission in writing from the publisher. Infringers of
copyright render themselves liable to prosecution.

ISBN 0 7900 0179 9
© 1991, John Connor
First published 1991
Printed in Singapore

Editorial services by Michael Gifkins and Associates

The publishers gratefully acknowledge
the assistance of the Literature Programme
of the Queen Elizabeth II Arts Council of New Zealand.

To Helene

CONTENTS

Nobazznobatrazz	1
Jonah	6
A Bit of Fishing	11
The Joker	18
Man of Fire	23
Show Home	31
Distortions	38

NOBAZZNOBATRAZZ

I COULD HAVE been a ghoul, a robber of graves, a cannibal. I was a boy with a bag full of eyes. When I opened it they gazed at me. They were blue and grey and green, like eyes should be. I put my hand amongst them and felt them roll between my fingers, clicking and rattling like the sounds of snooker through half-open doors.

I was an innocent abroad in a rude world. A British *Boy's Own Annual* cardboard cut-out, rosy-cheeked and runny-nosed. My sleeve glistened like a snail's trail. I had polished my shoes, pulled up my socks and washed behind my ears. My hair was slicked down with Brylcreem and sat like a greasy Belgian beret on my head. My tie was straight, my pockets were full of elastic bands, string and bubble-gum cards. I smiled full in the face of life. God was in his heaven and all was well with the world. I had a bag full of marbles and was ready to play the game.

'What's your name?' one of the boys asked. He was short, pug-faced and freckled and had an unattractive smile. I could see we were going to be friends.

'Tim,' I replied.

He scratched a circle on the ground with the heel of his shoe and we each placed a marble in it.

A boy with the expression and demeanour of one who has done something nasty in his trousers went first. He knelt on the ground, raised his eyes and recited very quickly, 'Nobazznobatrazz.'

Was he foreign? Hindu or Jew? I had heard of such things. No Christian would say what he said. The fear and fascination of outlandish people came over me as he flicked the marble. A poor shot, it was nowhere near the circle. Whatever supernatural power he had called on wasn't listening.

The pug-faced boy was next. His malevolent little eyes twinkled at me.

'Nobazznobatrazz.'

Him too. A stranger in a strange land, I watched as he flicked the marble. The obscene manner in which he did this increased my affection for him. He was better than the first boy and pocketed two marbles; one of them mine. Still, I didn't mind. It was a small price to pay for friendship.

'Your turn now,' he grinned at me.

It's as well in a foreign country to go along with some of the customs. I went to a Catholic church once to see what they got up to there. There was a lot of bobbing up and down on one knee, as if the string had gone in the other one. I did the same. It was the polite thing and I was a polite boy, brought up in a house that shone with polished brass.

I knelt down and hesitated.

'Nobazz . . .' but I'd forgotten the rest.

The boys screamed and cackled, their strange and savage glee accompanied by the accusation, 'He didn't say Nobatrazz.'

I was terrified. Torture of the fingertips was not unknown in these parts. I should have listened to my mother.

'Don't go down Rudyard Road,' she'd told me. 'There's bad company there.'

Bad company was, of course, exactly what I wanted so I defied her. How would I now explain the crooked tie, the torn shirt, the undone shoelaces, the missing fingernails and the slit nostrils?

None of these things happened. Instead, a supercilious boy with eyebrows to match walked over and behind the circle of marbles. He stood there, a judge, his long trousers the symbol of his authority.

'You didn't say Nobatrazz,' he pronounced.

'I forgot.'

This pathetic explanation was treated with the contempt it deserved. He stood feet together then slowly turned the toes of his shoes outwards. There was an art to this; an understanding of geometry and mechanics, vectors and gravity; a knowledge of physics beyond my comprehension. His shoes now presented a wall behind the circle so that no marbles could be knocked out. He pointed to his feet and sneered.

'Batrazz,' he said, and then slowly for my benefit, 'back racks.'

I was about to protest but then I hadn't said 'Nobatrazz.' I shrugged a resigned shrug and flicked my futile marble into the circle. The supercilious boy smirked and stepped back amongst his friends.

'It's your turn,' the pug-faced one announced, looking at me.
'But I've just gone.'
'You go twice. That's the rule.' And so it was. There was no arguing with a mind capable of that kind of logic.

'Nobatrazz,' I said as I prepared to flick the next marble.

Their glee was unparalleled by anything I had met so far; not that I was all that worldly. I had, later, the experience of braking suddenly on a grocery bicycle. The mirth of the bystanders as I bounced along the cross bar surpassed this glee, but only just.

'He didn't say Nobazz,' but the loss of another marble was worth the discovery of this mystery.

The 'bazz' of 'Nobazz' was easy. It consisted of the supercilious boy placing a suggestively large hand in front of the circle. 'Nobazz' equals 'No bars' and 'bars' simply bar your marble from entering the circle.

But I was happy. The double god was exposed. Nobazznobatrazz was discovered. I didn't realise that a host of demigods and demons lurked behind him, along with a whole litany of incantations. In my ignorance I felt a sense of brotherhood. The pug-faced boy was incorporated into fantasies of the future. We would build a den in the woods, and intrigue there against our enemies. I would invite him around to my place and he would meet my parents. They would be delighted with his dirty shoes and sullen ways. He would steal something, an ashtray or darning needle, and be treated with suspicion. I would be advised not to see him again. Then we would meet secretly, safe against our common foes. It was going to be so wonderful. Every time I spoke the word its magic was accepted and our friendship increased.

I lost more marbles but in an ecstasy of ritual the game continued.

I had one particularly beautiful marble, blue flecked with white, shiny and silent like the world from a million miles away. 'Nobazznobatrazz,' I cried as I flicked it into the circle.

It touched, delicately, another marble and stopped. The pug-faced boy, his eyes glistening with malicious joy, looked quickly at his supercilious partner.

'Drops,' proclaimed the supercilious boy in a sepulchral voice.

Eye drops? Ear drops for some pustular ailment? Chocolate drops? Not with these boys. Pear drops? Sharp and acid. Perhaps. I steeled myself as he put his hand in his pocket. No sticky, lint covered lolly appeared. Instead he drew out a silver orb, evil and hard amongst all this brittle glass. A ball-bearing 10 times the size of my little blue world.

'No drops,' I squeaked, but the pug-faced boy grinned and shook his head. It was too late. Again the supercilious boy demonstrated his grasp of mechanics; the forces that move planets smashed my marble to smithereens, and smithereens are very small indeed.

A corner of my slicked-down hair curled up like a piece of old linoleum. My tie came undone. My shoes were dirty, the laces untied. I was as crumpled as an empty cornflake packet left out in the rain for a fortnight. My marbles clanked and scraped together like condemned men. And so they went, one by one.

'Nobazznobatrazznodrops.' I was not aware of 'Hides'. The pug-faced boy merely picked up his marbles from the circle and put them in his pocket when it was my turn.

'Nobazznobatrazznodropsnohides.' No good. Among these sharp-toothed goblins was 'Stamps'. My marble was stamped on as it hurried towards the circle.

'I don't like this game. It's not fair.' The logic of my remarks was lost on them. I was bent on home with my few remaining marbles but I had not reckoned on 'Tweaks'.

My mother, nibbling her biscuits, would not understand. Crumbs would cling to her painted lips, the tea spill into the sugar bowl. Her bright and shining boy brought home in rags, exultant, and all his marbles gone.

JONAH

WE HAVE ENDED our last journey together. My friend is dead. The other night I sat at my journal: 'prawns' I wrote. That's what I had for dinner. I often do, but these prawns were different; the best I ever tasted.

We are far from home, far from the deep ocean. Out along the shore this morning people stood in their bright clothes. They waved and pointed. Many took photographs. Some came out in boats, but not too close. Soon I will be back amongst them. Most will not see me; most never did. I look like a man who has been through a long illness. My hair is white, my skin pale and mottled. If people want to know what happened I will tell them but I doubt they would want to come that close to something they do not understand.

The day I arrived it was as if I had been expected. There were tables and chairs, a bed, books everywhere, a desk, paper, ballpoint pens and a lamp kept burning all the time. There, hidden in his vast anatomy, a room was prepared for me.

That morning I had gone fishing. In an aluminium boat I had drifted far out in the Firth. Islands floated on the horizon and made me sleepy. That plus the beer, I suppose, though I never drink more than a bottle. I was wondering whether to try the handline when out of the sea a tail rose up as big and high as a roof-top. It slipped back into the water without a ripple. I should have been terrified but I wasn't. I stood in the boat and waited for something to happen, for something beyond my control to take over.

A flipper the size of a 747's wing caught the boat and tipped it over. My handlines, my bait, my tackle box and I fell tangled together into the sea and were swallowed by the whale. I should have died, churned up and turned to soup in its bowels, but I lived; I lived there with air to breathe and light to see, books to read and a stove to cook on.

There was room for them all. There were corridors and passageways hung with oil lamps. I spent hours, days at a time, exploring them. Such things are impossible, I know, but I learned not to question them. If I strayed from my reading late at night and wondered how a book could exist in such a place the print would melt and run off the page. If I wondered how the oil lamps kept burning, their light dimmed. If I stopped cooking to wonder how the prawns were brought to me there would be less of them in the pan. One awful day I wondered how I could live inside a whale and my fingers disappeared; I had to walk the corridors for hours before they decided to come back.

The day I learned that lesson I turned down a corridor and into a chamber where I could see out beyond the blubbery walls. We were on the surface of the sea, not far from land. Cars were slipping silently along the coast road and there was the flash of sunlight on windows, the grey roof of the car assembly plant and the Kopu Bridge made of matchsticks. We were back in the Firth. A feeling of dismay came over me — I wasn't ready to return.

As I watched, the land blurred and the whale sighed like a steam engine and dived. I ran along the corridors back to my room, sat in my chair and shut my eyes. I kept them shut but I didn't sleep; I tried to concentrate on the sea, to force the land away. When I opened my eyes I knew we were once more out in the deep ocean. I called out loud to the whale, 'Thank you.' Somewhere far above me, in a place beyond the reach of the corridors and passageways, he heard.

I told him things. Things I thought he would like to hear: how much I enjoyed the prawns, what good taste he had to swallow my favourite books, how thoughtful of him to keep the lamps burning and the stove supplied with oil and how, by some ingenious method, for all his plunging through the ocean he kept my room and the corridors steady; I never once fell over. He seemed to enjoy this. There were crayfish as well as prawns and the lamps burned brighter. I risked a criticism. I told him how much I missed fresh fruit. The next day he swallowed a box of Kerikeri oranges. He swallowed Rua potatoes, cauliflowers, peas and kumara. I lived like a king and was happy. I thought of the ocean outside full of sharks and squids, rays and stinging jellyfish. The ocean could be raging or silent but it never came down the corridors and into my room.

There was the chamber where I could see out, but until the last few weeks, when things started to go wrong, I rarely went there. Sometimes, though, on my journeys along the corridors, I would turn a corner and find myself in the chamber. Once I saw the tip of Taranaki above the flat clouds and thought perhaps the land might not be so bad after all, but then I saw the chemical chimneys of Motunui. Another day the snaggle-toothed Whangarei Heads gave me the same idea until I saw the poison works of Marsden Point. Each time I ran to my room and shut my eyes until we were far out in the ocean again. I was safe there.

I walked the corridors, I read, I slept, I ate. I gave up keeping time; I had no need of it. I was happy. Then things started to go wrong. One day we came to the coast of the Coromandel. I ran to my room as usual and shut my eyes but when I opened them I knew we were still close to land. I shouted in anger. I complained. I demanded to be taken to the ocean where I belonged but the whale wouldn't listen. I stayed in my room and sulked. I refused to eat; the prawns and the goldfruit rotted where he left them. Still we stayed close to the coast. I saw people for the first time in years, fishing not a mile from us. They whipped their outboard in a frenzy to get away. I wanted the whale to smash them but he would never do that.

At last he took pity on me, or maybe he just changed his mind. In any case we left for the deep ocean that night. I thought it would be a return to normal but something far worse happened. At the end of one of the corridors the following day I saw a man. I tried not to believe in him and hoped he would waver and disappear like the lamps or the books but he stayed. He saw me and came towards me, a smile on his face as if he recognised a friend. I ran along corridors and passageways I had never explored before. I tried to find somewhere to hide but no matter where I ran I always ended up back in my room. I hid behind the bed. I shut my eyes but it didn't work. We were out in the ocean and the man wouldn't go away. I saw him every day of these last few weeks; every day except today. He smiled whenever he saw me. I had to force myself not to talk to him. I knew something terrible would happen if I as much as said a word.

A week ago I sat and ate a batch of green-lipped mussels. They were small and sweet. I picked at a strand of flesh caught in my teeth. It must have diverted me for a moment. When I returned to the plate, half the mussels had gone. The man sat opposite.

'Thank you,' he said. 'They were delicious.'

I was on the point of shouting at him when I stopped myself. I shut my eyes tight and made him go away but he was back again at breakfast. He read over my shoulder and greeted me in the corridors. He ate half my food and talked incessantly about things that had nothing to do with the whale or the ocean.

'Do you like the mince?' he asked as I ate a plate of pipis.

'Why did you come here?'

'How can we help you?'

I never answered him. I shut my eyes and made him go away, but he always came back. He talked of what a big place it was; how a person could get lost. He talked nonsense; about bus trips to Taranaki and Whangarei. He put things in my food that made me sleepy. He walked the corridors with me. I tried to avoid him by quickly darting up passageways but this only brought me to the chamber where I could see out. The whale was getting closer to the land; I ran to my room and shut my eyes but he didn't go back to the ocean. He cruised slowly past Great Barrier Island and the tip of the Coromandel. If I hid in my room the man would be there, softly talking to me. It was nonsense, all of it.

'There is no whale,' he said. 'There never has been.'

I hated him. When he sat the other night cracking a crayfish leg I told him to get out and leave me alone. They were the only words I spoke to him, but they were enough. He smiled and left. The lamps in the corridors dimmed and disappeared. I ate my last meal in the whale: prawns, the best I ever tasted.

This afternoon not many people watched from the shore. The whale was hardly a foot above the surface. His tail, once capable of forcing him clear of the water, had now only enough power to move him slowly into the Waihou Stream. The man had gone. I went to my room. The furniture was falling apart like soggy cardboard, the oil stove cold and dusty. Water full of prawn shells slopped about my ankles. A wave surged through it and I fell backwards as the whale crashed into the Kopu Bridge. Late tonight I felt my way along the unlit corridors to the whale's mouth. I had never dared go there before. Everything was quiet and the whale didn't move as I stepped out between his teeth.

A BIT OF FISHING

SHE WAS IN the jungle, stretched out on the limb of a tree like a cat. She was enticing, inviting. Her hair was black, her nails were red and her skin was green all over. Stephen gazed at the picture and tried not to think of the sea.

'If I had a woman like that,' Barry nudged him and grinned.

Liz came in and took his grin away, back-heeling the door shut behind her. She had a ballpoint pen between her teeth, a box file in one arm and little Samantha hanging on the other.

'Busy?' asked Barry and with Liz glaring at him took the box file off her.

A bell rang in the corner of the room and a car horn sounded. Outside, a utility with a trailer and aluminium dinghy at the back waited impatiently by the pumps. Liz pulled the pen from between her teeth.

'We can hear the bloody bell, you know.'

'Bloody,' said Samantha and waited for a reaction. Liz took a squashed licorice allsort from her apron pocket and gave it to her.

'Is that Hayden's ute?' Barry called from the back room.

'Who else drives a purple ute around here?'

'With his boat on the back?'

'Looks like it.' Liz sighed and shook her head. The car horn sounded again and she clenched her fists.

'I'll get it,' said Stephen.

She unclenched her fists. 'Thanks, Steve. I'm not in the mood for Hayden right now. Or any other time for that matter,' she added as Stephen closed the ranchslider door behind him.

'New at the job?' Hayden said as Stephen squeezed the release too soon and slopped petrol over the side of the jerry can.

'Just helping out.' Stephen tried a friendly smile on him but

Hayden remained expressionless. 'I'm down for the long weekend.'

'Long weekend.' Hayden dismissed the idea with a contemptuous snort. Suddenly, with the jerry can only half full he tapped the side of it with his boot.

'That'll do,' he said.

Stephen relaxed his grip on the handle.

'I thought you wanted it filled up.'

'Did I say that?' Hayden asked as if he had been accused.

'No,' Stephen admitted. 'I just thought . . .' but Hayden stopped him with a loud sigh.

'Put it on the account,' he said, screwing down the cap on the jerry can. 'Hayden.' He lifted the can into the dinghy.

Stephen tried to think of something cutting to say.

'I won't charge for spillage,' he attempted, but it was too late. Hayden had already slammed the utility door shut, and drove off, dinghy and trailer laughing maliciously behind.

'Uncle Steve said bastard,' Samantha announced and waited for another licorice allsort.

Liz gave her one.

'There are times when it's warranted,' she said.

Samantha stopped chewing, frowned and nodded wisely.

Out of the window and over the flat farmland and the hills of the Coromandel coast beyond, the sky was clear with not a breath of wind. The mangroves started across the road and followed the banks of the Piako River in a dark green line out to the Firth where the sea began and the sea-lice crawled in the soft grey mud, past raggedy worms with rasping teeth and jellyfish like ghosts. A big boat with dials and wheels and windows and vinyl seats was the answer. The more man-made things you could surround yourself with at sea, the safer you were.

'What sort of boat has Noel got?' Stephen asked, glad to hear the sound of his own voice.

'A dinghy,' said Liz. 'Same as Hayden's.'

A piece of tin with an outboard on the back.

'Oh,' said Stephen, as if he had asked an idle question and wasn't all that interested in the answer.

Barry, sitting on the lounge, grimaced as he pulled the top off a beer can.

'Do you think Hayden's going out again?' he asked and took a quick sip of the beer as it frothed out of the can.

'Why not?' Liz said. 'It's been over six months since Gerry drowned.'

As if that wasn't bad enough, Noel's boat was hardly more than a handspan above the waterline. Stephen sat in the prow facing forward and tried not to look uncomfortable; the story of Hayden's brother was still in his mind.

'Lost overboard in a squall while they were out fishing,' Barry told him and added, 'When Hayden came back and told everyone what had happened he didn't seem to care, carried on as usual, until Gerry's body was washed up on the Miranda mudflats three days later and Hayden had to identify it, or what was left of it.' On his second can by then, Barry would have been happy to go into more detail if Liz hadn't told him to keep quiet.

'Relax.' Noel was loping about in fisherman's boots, arranging bits of tackle.

'I'm OK,' Stephen said over his shoulder.

'She'll stay up without you holding her,' Noel said and pulled the cord on the outboard. Stephen took his hands off the side of the boat, folded them then unfolded them and felt like throwing them into the river but scratched the back of his head instead. Another pull on the cord and the outboard started. He grabbed the gunwale as the boat shook itself and turned into the stream. With the outboard gurgling and the dinghy moving slowly through the still water the waves rolled away smooth and round and glistening. Stephen thought if he fell overboard he would stick on the surface like a fly on syrup.

'Come down and do a bit of fishing,' Liz had said. 'Get out of yourself. You spend too much time up in your head.'

Before he had time to think about it she said, 'I'll fix it. You can go with Noel.'

Lazing about on the river and perhaps catching a fish was a pleasant thought, though. Unfortunately Noel wasn't a pipe-smoking dreamer. He made his living catching fish and was intent on showing his skills; going out to sea where the snapper were.

'Catch bugger-all in the river,' he said.

Still, so far it was lazy enough, with the boat chuckling away and the water quiet and smooth.

'Could get a bit choppy,' Noel said and eased the boat around a bend.

'A bit choppy?' There was barely a wind and no cloud.

Noel frowned knowledgeably up at the sky.

'Later,' he said.

Great. Just great. And this boat with all the power and strength of a milk-bottle top. Stephen refused to grip the side again when Noel opened up the throttle. The engine roared its disapproval but with the whip on it thrashed about and lifted the bow above the water. He was forced to hang on as the boat skidded along the surface, out of the river, and belly-flopped into the Firth where the waves smacked into it. Noel eased the throttle back and the engine settled into a steady growl. Stephen stopped gritting his teeth.

'I see what you mean,' he shouted above the noise of the outboard.

'Eh?' Noel relaxed with a smile on his face and the outboard arm resting under his hand.

Stephen swivelled around to face him like a fellow man of the sea.

'Choppy.'

Noel's smile widened and he laughed. 'Yeah,' he said, 'It's choppy all right.'

At least he had spared Stephen the nonsense of saying it was flat as a mill-pond because it wasn't. It was definitely not flat. Stephen leaned down to straighten his rod and reel which had fallen diagonally across the boat. Noel had three or four thick ugly handlines thrown about haphazardly. And naturally he would catch a dozen or more snapper where Stephen with his fancy equipment would be lucky to catch a sprat.

'We've a way to go yet,' Noel said as Stephen turned to face the waves again.

A way to go yet. Out to where the water was deeper; where a squall could blow up at any time. There was a definite wind now but Stephen said nothing and saved Noel dismissing it as a gentle breeze. It was sufficient to break the tops of the waves, though. The boat pitched into them and sent up spray to land on Stephen's lips. A rogue wave lifted up the boat and smacked it down. He had his eyes screwed tight shut, waiting for the boat to tip over or fill with water and sink like a leaf, slowly back and forth, to settle without a sound on the mud below.

He should have insisted on life-jackets. But nobody had mentioned life-jackets. A life-jacket would have meant you were frightened of death and out here with the salty, grim-faced men of the sea no one was frightened of death. But even with a life-jacket your legs dangled temptingly in the water with God knows what sharp-toothed horror lurking below, ready to saw you in half.

When he opened his eyes the spray hit them. He turned around in the seat again. There was water in the bottom of the boat now, running up and down in a frenzy of indecision. Stephen's shoes were soaked. Noel's eyes were gleaming. He grinned as he rode the waves. The Bronco Billy of the high seas. Behind him the line of mangroves was nothing but a grey-green smudge on the horizon. Away to the left only the houses on the high ground of Thames were visible; the rest had disappeared over the rim of the earth.

'How much further?' Stephen said.

Noel frowned at him as if he wasn't sure what kind of fish he was looking at.

'Another hour,' he said.

An hour. It was too much. If this was Liz's plan to get him out of himself it wasn't working. Stephen was in his head again, but not in the library where he worked. He was down in the cellar where the nightmares squeaked and chattered and scampered about.

'Bastard!' Noel shouted suddenly.

Stephen dashed up the cellar steps prepared to defend himself but Noel was stretching up from his seat and peering over Stephen's shoulder.

'That bloody Hayden!'

Stephen half turned and looked to where Noel was pointing.

'I can't see anything,' he said.

'That's his boat.' Noel sat down and aimed the boat at Hayden's. 'Away for months and the first thing he does is poach.'

Stephen could see Hayden's boat now; about half a mile away and low in the water. It was bobbing and slewing about. There was no one on board.

'Where is he?' he asked.

Noel eased off the throttle and the boat shuddered.

'I don't know,' he said.

Stephen stood up as they circled Hayden's boat but Noel told him to sit down. When they came alongside Noel held the two boats together with a gaff. Dozens of snapper in the bottom of Hayden's boat stared at Stephen with their sunken jelly eyes. Noel found the anchor in the middle of them and threw it out, muttering to himself, 'Poacher,' then in a louder voice,'We better start looking for him.'

Stephen stood up and looked for Hayden. He would be floating face down, arms stretched out, crucified on the sea. He tried to tell himself he didn't want to see it. He was too sensitive, cultured and civilised, but he almost fell overboard in his eagerness to be the first to glimpse the body.

'You wouldn't be so keen if you'd ever seen a drowned man,' said Noel.

Stephen shifted his footing to steady himself and tried to avoid Noel's eyes.

'It's in us all,' said Noel and pushed away from Hayden's boat.

Stephen felt a twinge of disappointment when he saw Hayden waving to him on Noel's third sweep around the dinghy. They came alongside him and Noel hauled him aboard with one hand.

Hayden sat there with his arms wrapped around his knees, shivering and dripping wet.

'Give him your jacket,' Noel ordered and headed the boat back to Hayden's. Stephen stopped staring; he took off his waterproof jacket and put it around Hayden's shoulders.

'What happened?' he asked, surprised Noel hadn't asked first.

Hayden looked up from his bare feet and smiled at some private bad joke.

'I thought I'd take a little walk,' he said.

'Like Gerry,' said Noel, staring hard at the back of Hayden's head. Hayden looked around quickly then sullenly turned away to gaze across the waves.

'I thought if I came out and faced it I'd be all right. I thought I was too; working like old times and no Gerry to bother me, but he started calling for me again.'

'He's dead,' said Noel coldly.

Stephen, on the cellar steps, heard a rattle at the door and his nightmares stopped their chatter. He looked to Noel for help but Noel was careful not to meet his eyes as he opened up the throttle on the outboard. Hayden raised his voice above the wind and the outboard's growl.

'I went looking for him this time.' He slowly shook his head.

Noel said nothing. He cut the engine and coasted alongside Hayden's boat.

Stephen pushed his shoulder against the cellar door and, with his hand shaking, turned the key in the lock. Hayden was on the other side, kicking and banging his fist against the door.

'He wouldn't let me join him,' he said and pulled the jacket closer around his shoulders. 'He wants me alive so he can watch me like he has done since the day they made me look at him.'

Noel hauled up the anchor and secured Hayden's boat to his.

Stephen backed away from the cellar door. He was about to scurry across to his own flimsy nightmares cowering in the corner but Hayden suddenly turned from the waves, kicked the door wide open and looked straight at him.

'He has no eyes,' he said, 'but he watches me. Don't you understand?'

THE JOKER

I HAVE JUST returned from viewing my work. It has taken all day to arrange the chemical apparatus but from the street below it looks splendid. The green liquid in the retort is particularly effective. I stood against the shadow of a wall and watched a small group of people gather. They looked up at my window and remarked on the Erlenmeyer flask, the bell jars, thistle funnels, test tubes and retort. It was gratifying to hear one of them suggest that the green liquid might be poison. It is nothing of the sort. It is vegetable dye. Tomorrow I shall burn magnesium for them. The brightness and shadows will be good for their imaginations and this record evidence of their folly.

The magnesium was a great success. The shadows I made as I crept about were as horrible as goblins. My greatest success today, however, was an accident. I was rehearsing a scene for the evening's performance and had the blind pulled down. I was undecided whether to peer into the Erlenmeyer flask or to pour something suspiciously red into the retort. As I picked up the flask and pondered, the blind flew up. A slovenly girl pushing a shopping trolley noticed me from the street. I glared at her in exasperation, interrupted in my rehearsal, but the quick look of fear before she hurried away told me I had been discovered at one of my 'secret experiments'. I will use that trick again.

The woman has been. I call her a woman though she is far too young. Her hair is medieval, fair as a maiden's should be, yet what did those maidens think of, tied in flimsy chains with dragons seething at their feet? Whatever it was, it wasn't overseas trips and pot plants. Still, she is concerned about me and is paid six dollars an hour to be so. She asked me questions: am I eating, drinking, sleeping well?

'Oh yes I am, and keeping regular too. I have taken your advice about the high-fibre diet. Why, there's more fibre in me than a hessian sack.'

She laughed when I told her that. She asked about my chemical apparatus, searching so prettily for a delusion or two. I told her it was for experiments in the study of the mind. She appeared satisfied. It also had more mundane uses, I explained, and poured a decoction into a flask for her. It was herbal tea. She politely declined my offer with a look of apprehension. As I put down the flask the blind flew up and the same slovenly girl passed in the street.

Today has been a triumph. Early this morning I purchased a live piglet. Pink and squealing, it was perfect for my purposes. I took it back to my room, carefully so as not to be seen, and dressed it in a frilly bonnet and my own christening shawl. It was quiet, even content, in its disguise until I pinched its fat little belly when it squealed beautifully. I placed it under my coat where it soon quietened down again.

At the shops by the bus-stop there was a push-chair with a pretty little baby in it. I am dismayed by mothers who leave their babies unattended like this. They do it all the time. Don't they know there are maniacs about? I waited for more people to gather at the bus-stop and made as if to admire the baby, bending closer to do so. Then I gave my piglet a good pinch and ran past the horrified queue, the piglet squealing, its bonnet and shawl plain for all to see.

Of course the truth would quickly be established and just as quickly forgotten, the rumours less quick but best remembered. A practical joker or a stealer of infants? The latter will prevail, I think.

When I returned to my room I undressed the piglet, then released it in the garden. It sniffed at the rhododendrons then trotted off as a piglet ought. There are many hereabouts who will take care of it one way or another. Its future is of no concern to me.

My evening's performance was, as usual, a success, but I am

tiring of it. I think something of an electrical nature, something which hums and sparks, would keep them guessing. As I mused on this and sipped my herbal tea, a terrible squealing, or rather screaming, came up from my garden. It was high and surprised then snapped off like a switch. I thought my piglet had returned and, though the sudden termination of its cries was evidence of its capture, I went down to the garden to make sure it had gone. The ground near the rhododendrons had been disturbed. Whoever caught it must have waited until he thought I was asleep. He need not have worried himself. The piglet's welfare is, as I have said, no concern of mine. Still, a scream in the night is quite effective and can only add to my reputation. I thank him for that.

It was the woman's day for visiting today. I had proposed to demonstrate my dynamo to her. It develops a charge which jumps across the terminals like an electric worm, but she didn't come. In the privacy of this record I confess I am disappointed. She is a fraud, of course, and cares no more for me than I care for her, but she means well I suppose. Perhaps she will come tomorrow? Perhaps she is at home nursing an ailing aspidistra or a moribund maidenhair? Whatever, it is of no importance to me.

The evening's performance did not go well. Only a few people watched from the street and there was a disturbing sullenness about them.

I turned off the dynamo earlier than I had planned and was vaguely depressed as I pulled down the blind.

Against my usual custom I am writing in the morning. I read what I had written yesterday and noticed a distinct melancholy about it. For honesty's sake I will not throw it away. It is what I wrote and so it stays. Yet it is, how shall I put it, a most unusual drizzle in the otherwise sunny climate of my mind. I will busy myself today and perfect an explosion for this evening's performance. Lots of noise and smoke is called for.

The performance this evening was cancelled. Its absence will excite their curiosity so nothing is lost, but I had not planned it that way. The melancholy mood of yesterday has not gone; it is compounded. I have been visited by the police, two polite but persistent men. Their manner was respectful and they seemed eager to learn from me. Their enquiries were 'just routine'. They actually used that phrase. The woman is missing; she has disappeared. 'What of it?' I said. 'People have a right to disappear if they so choose.' 'Quite so,' they agreed. Their enquiries, they repeated, were 'just routine'. She had left a message that she might pop in to see me on her way home. When I informed them that she had not 'popped in' they left. They did not seem satisfied but I suppose that is a trick they use to worry the guilty.

A most unusual and disturbing thing. One of my chief delights is to hide in the philosophy section of the library. It is a lonely and rarely visited place. I peer between the volumes of Wittgenstein and Heidegger and wait for women to gather around the romantic novels. Then I emerge, a figure of power and suspicion. They invariably draw to one side and stop their chatter. I like to hear their excited whispers when they think I have gone but today there was that same sullenness I had felt two nights ago, as if they wished me ill. With contemptible courage one of them spoke, loud enough for me to hear.

'Murderer,' she said.

I have cancelled this evening's performance again.

A dreadful event. The woman has been murdered. The police called again, their attitude one of subdued awe. It was as if they had cornered a dangerous animal, but what danger am I? A small danger maybe, if it is dangerous to unsettle people, but I am not a murderer. They asked about my apparatus. The woman was drugged before she died, they said. The only thing I make with it is herbal tea. Extravagant for tea, they said, and so it is. Its true purpose, I explained, is to investigate the human mind, but now I wish I hadn't told them. They reminded me of her intention to visit me and I repeated that no such visit took place. A woman answering her description was seen near this house on the night in question. Though their object was to trap me I was amused by their phrases: 'answering her description', 'night in question'. Yet again I was forced to repeat that she did not visit, did not 'pop in'. Then there was the scream. In their peculiar mechanical way they continued, 'A sound resembling a woman's scream was heard to come from the vicinity of your garden.' I explained about the piglet but they were far from convinced. 'There are signs of a struggle having taken place by the rhododendrons. Was it a big piglet?' they asked.

'No,' I replied, 'Only small,' though I hardly noticed their question. Some days ago I accused the woman of being a fraud but it is I who am the fraud. I am none of the things I pretend to be; a poisoner, a kidnapper, an experimenter in forbidden knowledge, sipping herbal tea and congratulating myself on my reputation for evil. What do I know of evil?

When the police left they called me sir but I could sense their frustration. They suspect me; well, I am suspicious, but their evidence is circumstantial. I will cease my performances and other tricks for a while, at least until this business is over. I have no wish to provide them with further evidence.

Could it be that I am afraid, that I have always been afraid? Perhaps that is why I carried out my pranks; in the belief that I could fool them, but all the while afraid of them, fooling no one. If the woman was here she could explain it, but she isn't here.

Early this morning I sat looking at my chemical apparatus. Someone threw a brick through my window and smashed my retort. As I picked up the pieces another brick smashed the Erlenmeyer flask and test tubes. I stood up expecting to see whoever it was running away, but he was still there, hatred on his face and another brick in his hand.

MAN OF FIRE

IN 1904 WHEN I was a boy my father took me from Beachlands to Auckland on the back of a horse to see John Lieby.

'If you behave yourself,' he told me, 'I'll take you to see the famous Man of Fire.'

So I behaved myself. It wasn't difficult. I was better behaved than most boys my age.

Beachlands was a small place then, not like now. Within a day of my father telling me, everyone knew we were off to see the Man of Fire. Most had seen him already and their eyes glowed when they spoke of him. 'A wonderful man,' they said. 'A miracle worker.'

Uncle Seth said John Lieby was a fake and my mother shushed him angrily as if he had sworn. She needn't have bothered, though. I didn't believe Uncle Seth. To him everyone was a fake including himself. Besides, my father proved him wrong by showing me a handbill. It was bent in one corner where the flap of his pocket had caught it and read:

MR J. LIEBY

INVITES YOU TO WATCH HIM

BURN

AT AUCKLAND TOWN HALL

5 PM AUGUST 16TH 1904

ADMISSION: 1 SHILLING AND 6 PENCE

On the day we left Beachlands a small crowd of well-wishers gathered.

'Good luck,' they said and my father leaned down from our horse, Daphne, to shake their hands.

'Good luck, Tommy.' One or two waved to me as we set off

down Mill Street. We rounded the corner at McKechnie's Dairy where some of my school-mates slouched around the hitching rail and stared at us. I smirked at them, my heart full of contempt and adventure. Waiheke Island across the water shone in the brilliant winter light. We cantered along the beachfront and wheeled right, into the open country. I held my arms tight around my father's waist and pressed my cheek against the back of his corduroy coat. He smelt of tobacco and beer. Loose change chinked in his pocket. There would be a Chelsea bun and a cup of tea at Howick for sure.

My father reined Daphne in as we passed Mad Dan Arnett's farm. Mad Dan at his gate shouted, 'Give the bastard one for me.'

He shouted it to everyone.

'Too right, Dan,' my father replied and Mad Dan laughed.

I lifted my head from my father's coat and felt the corduroy ruts in my cheek.

'All right, son?' he asked.

'Too right,' I said and he laughed.

At Whitford word had preceded us. Mrs Seaton, the postmistress, beckoned us to stop as we galloped up the hill from Turangi Creek. Daphne halted as she always did at the top of the hill. My father tipped his hat back, took a white-spotted red handkerchief from his top pocket and wiped his brow.

'Off to see Whitford's famous son?' Mrs Seaton beamed at us as if she herself had given birth to John Lieby.

'Indeed we are, Mrs Seaton,' my father answered with the formality due a local official.

'First time, young Tom?' She turned her beam towards me.

'Too right,' I said but this time my father didn't laugh.

Mrs Seaton momentarily switched off her beam but quickly switched it on again.

'He was born right there.' She pointed to a squat house across the road. Its low verandah scowled at me.

'It was there that his great gift was made known to us.'

Her eyes looked into the past. 'He could light up the sky for miles around in those days or turn himself down to a dull glow, just enough to do your toast on.' She smiled a brief smile and was back in the present. 'I won't keep you,' she said. 'You've a long journey ahead.'

Although she wasn't in our way she stood to one side to let us know we could go.

My father tapped Daphne gently in the flanks with his heels.

'Good day, Mrs Seaton.' He touched the brim of his hat. I turned in the saddle and waved.

'Don't believe all you hear about him,' she called after us.

'I won't,' I shouted back, bouncing up and down in time with Daphne. And I didn't either. Already I didn't believe her story of sitting around John Lieby's glowing body making toast. I asked my father if he thought it was true. He'd heard the story before and said it was the sort of story Whitford people would make up.

'They're a tight-fisted lot,' he added, as if that explained it.

By mid-afternoon we made Otahuhu where our travelling companion went his separate way. His name was Mr Cuthbertson.

'A traveller in women's undergarments,' he told us and leered at me when we met him in the Howick Tea House. My father tried to put him off with a curt nod but Mr Cuthbertson didn't take the hint. He stood with his cup at an angle slopping tea into his saucer and spoke with his mouth full of egg and lettuce sandwich.

'Old John Lieby,' he mumbled and sprayed bits of half-chewed sandwich across the table top. He righted his cup and sat down beside me. He smelt of rotten talcum powder and swallowed noisily.

'I knew him in his heyday.'

'His days are still hey as far as I'm concerned,' my father said.

Mr Cuthbertson frowned then smiled. 'Yes, yes of course they are.'

He accompanied us to Otahuhu and when we stopped by the track along the way he sat with us and told us lies.

'I saw him once in the days before his fame spread,' he sneered at me. 'He was crackling away nicely by the shores of Lake Taupo.'

My father lit the end of a roll-your-own and spat a piece of tobacco off his lower lip. Mr Cuthbertson raised his eyebrows but quickly brought them down again. He stared forlornly at the ground and said, 'I wasn't always in women's undergarments, you know.'

At the stop before Otahuhu Mr Cuthbertson behaved in an unforgivable manner.

My father lit a fire and made billy tea. Mr Cuthbertson, uninvited, joined us and brought his suitcase with him. After he had drunk our tea he opened the suitcase and rummaged about among the rivets and fastenings of his trade.

'There,' he announced and took out a pair of scissors big enough to stab someone with. He tugged his forelock and with the scissors snipped it off then flung it on the fire. It sizzled up and disappeared.

'Utterly destroyed,' he said. 'Burnt out of existence.'

There was no denying it. My father and I nodded in agreement.

'Then why is it that John Lieby lives?' Mr Cuthbertson demanded. 'He burns but he is not consumed. Not a hair on his macassared head is harmed.'

My father tipped the dregs of his tea on the fire and in the hiss of rising steam said, 'It's a mystery to me.'

'Me too,' I said and Mr Cuthbertson glared at me.

Through the Tamaki mangroves he tried to persuade us to his thinking.

'It's a hallucination,' he insisted as his horse, Robert, sank up to his fetlocks in the mangrove mud.

'Hallucinations don't burn toast,' my father called over his shoulder.

The only answer we received was the slurp of Robert's hooves in the mud.

Disgusted, Mr Cuthbertson left us at Otahuhu.

As we rode through the town red-cheeked women in bright floral aprons nodded to us from their tumbledown verandahs.

Out beyond the Penrose swamp the sheep in the holding pens stopped in mid-chew to ponder us. Daphne kept her head down and cringed past them.

At Newmarket, my father halted for a beer. I stayed outside and kept Daphne company. All around, on the walls and the shop windows, were posters advertising the Man of Fire; the same as the handbill only bigger and brighter and with one addition. Below the admission price was written, 'His Farewell Performance'.

'Your first and last sight of a man to tell your grandchildren about,' my father said and lifted me onto Daphne's back.

We stabled Daphne at Fogarty's (sixpence a day or part thereof). It's gone now like so many other things and a concrete box is in its place. It was early evening when we climbed the hill above Fogarty's and beheld Auckland Town clattering and rolling its way down through the gaslights to Queen Street. The verandahs and hitching rails were festooned with red and yellow bunting fluttering like flames in the breeze. The whole town was on fire for John Lieby. Street-sellers in torn-brim hats sold souvenirs from trays held by straps across their shoulders. The souvenirs were mostly teacloths and handkerchiefs with not very life-like pictures of the Man of Fire printed on them. My father, who was experienced in these matters, sought out one particular souvenir. It appeared to be a simple wooden model about six inches high of a man in a black frock-coat and top hat. He stood on a small plinth. Out of the crown of his top hat grew a short piece of string and a longer one from the bottom of the plinth. If you held the plinth and pulled the top string the man burst into flame, or so it seemed. Pulling the string had the effect of letting fly open tiny hinged panels spaced throughout the frock-coat. Their undersides were painted bright yellow, orange and red.

The street-seller grinned lasciviously as he allowed John Lieby to twirl on the end of the string. My father, without complaining, bought the model for three shillings and gave it to me. I have it to this day and sometimes show it to my great-grandchildren, to intrigue them. When I tell them there really was such a man they don't believe me, such is the scepticism of today's youth. In my day I would have believed anything.

By the time we were half-way down Wellesley Street I had set fire to John Lieby a dozen times and more. Whenever I turned off the flames, though, the expression on his face became more angry, but sad as well, as if I had no right to amuse myself at his expense. I stopped playing with him and asked my father to take him. He smiled and put him in his haversack.

We had seats at the front of the Town Hall with nothing between us and the edge of the stage but a row of potted palms. People greeted each other too loudly and laughed too heartily. Someone kicked the flimsy legs of my fold-up chair. My father patted my arm.

'Patience,' he said and winked.

The lights dimmed and the audience settled; only one or two snipers firing off a last cough. We could hear the muffled protests of those people outside who had left it too late. Then the curtains opened to reveal a military band which struck up immediately and played patriotic Empire tunes.

'The Governor's here,' my father muttered and set his face against the music.

The band hurried on to the National Anthem and everyone shuffled to their feet. As I had learned the chorus at school I started to sing but my father tapped my shoulder to keep me quiet. The music finished and we all sat down. The Governor, to our right and above us in the gallery, remained standing a while longer, smiling to acknowledge the meagre applause. Then he sat down and quickly buried his head in his programme. We hadn't come to see him.

The band marched off and John Lieby marched on. He turned to face us and caught sight of my open mouth. I closed it and John Lieby nodded his approval. To our left a woman sank in her chair and nearly disappeared inside her numerous skirts. Friends on either side hurriedly propped her up again.

Even without a top hat John Lieby was as tall as a chimney. His black coat went straight down without a wrinkle from his shoulders almost to his ankles. He wore black polished boots and above his head a circle of blue flame hovered. When he brushed a lock of hair from his forehead, yellow pilot flames flickered at his fingertips. And this Man of Fire spoke to us of snow.

'You,' he spoke softly but accused us, 'have come to see me burn.'

'Burn.' The prayer went up around me.

'But I dream of snow.'

'Snow,' we whispered.

'I have always dreamed of snow.' As he spoke his coat lapels and pocket flaps caught fire. His voice went over our heads and caught the people in the far gallery and rear stalls.

'Snow,' they sighed and his brass buttons glowed red.

'In my dreams,' he narrowed his eyes, 'I hear it falling softly at night.'

Ribbons of fire twined around his arms and criss-crossed across his coat.

'And in its strange cold silence,' he looked down in dismay at his blazing sleeves, 'I know I am not on fire.'

But we could see that he was. The front of his boots burst open and snarled through the flames like new-born dragons. My father gripped my hand but his gaze was fixed on John Lieby.

'Snow is a beautiful thing,' my father murmured.

'Snow is a beautiful thing,' John Lieby said and raised his arm like a torch before him. 'I long for it.'

I had never seen snow but I longed for it too. We all did. But our longings were nothing compared to John Lieby's. He dropped his hand disconsolately to his side and the coughing started. The people in the gallery were most affected; the Governor worst of all. His tongue curled up tight and flicked in and out of his purple face. Those around him waved and coughed and held handkerchiefs to their eyes.

'It's the smoke from John Lieby's clothes,' my father explained and grinned at the Governor's discomfort.

'It'll soon be gone.'

It was, and with it John Lieby's clothes. Several of the women in our row sighed and swooned (an art women seem to have lost since the Great War). No one but me took any notice of them.

My father was on his feet together with other men and those women who hadn't fainted. I rose too, my mouth and eyes wide open.

John Lieby blazed in abject triumph before us, his shoulders slumped and his body wrapped in fire. Though I live to be a hundred, which is not likely given my present state of health, I doubt if I will ever see again a sight as awesome as that. An ordinary man would have turned to crackling and died but John Lieby was untouched. Though every part of it was on fire, his body was not harmed and the pain he felt was not physical. His voice dropped but we could hear him still.

'I can never, never feel the comfort of snow.'

SHOW HOME

A TIGHT-HAIRED representative met them at the door. When she spoke Stuart noticed spots of lipstick on her teeth.

'Good morning,' she said. Her eyes flicked back and forth from Stuart to Amelia. 'If you'd care to wait a while?' She indicated a seat inside the hallway. 'For the traffic to die down.' She gave a quick laugh. 'There are so many young couples coming through.'

Stuart saw a carousel of couples circling the dining room table.

'One of our more popular homes,' the representative explained. 'Perhaps you would care to peruse our brochure while you wait?'

'Yes please.' Amelia took one of the polished pamphlets off the table near the doorway. The representative smoothed down an already smoothed-down collar and smiled at another young couple crunching their way up the gravel path.

Stuart looked at the artist's impression of the house on the front of the pamphlet. It was an accurate enough drawing, he supposed. There was the house: straight lines, sharp points and windows everywhere. There was the birch tree with its delicate fleck of leaves and there was Stuart and Amelia, sketched quickly, a dozen strokes of the pen each, he with his arm around her, she side on, looking at him or the house. It was hard to tell which.

'Come on,' Amelia said. 'The traffic's died down.'

Stuart looked across at the representative who nodded at them to begin their inspection. Amelia took Stuart's arm and headed into the lounge room. It was a jungle. Half hidden amongst the ferns and philodendra, the ivy and the aspidistras, were leather armchairs gathered around a glistening glass table. There were thin white splotches on the rubber plant near

Stuart's left arm. He wet his thumb and tried to clean one of the leaves. It soon dried out but the splotch remained.

'Don't do that, Stuart,' Amelia nudged him. 'Someone might see.' She made for one of the leather chairs.

'It's a waste of time anyway.' Stuart trudged after her. He stopped with his back to one of the chairs, about to sit down.

'Don't,' Amelia whispered loudly.

'What now?' He straightened up quickly.

'Look.' Amelia bent down next to Stuart and twanged a thin piece of cord strung across the arms of the chair. 'To stop people like you,' she said. 'They're such beautiful chairs.' She wiped one of the arms where Stuart's hand had been.

'Not fit for the likes of me,' Stuart muttered. He flicked at something on top of the glass table. His thumbnail made a tiny snapping noise and Amelia glared at him.

'I thought it was a hair,' he said, 'but it's a crack.'

'Well leave it alone,' Amelia snapped. 'You know,' she stepped back and smiled, 'this lounge room is perfect. It's just how I'd like our lounge room to be.'

'Perfect,' Stuart said, 'if you like spotty pot plants, chairs you can't sit down in and broken table tops.'

Amelia lowered her voice. 'Don't start, please.'

'I wasn't starting.' Stuart looked at the pamphlet. 'Come on,' he said. 'There's a high-tech kitchen somewhere.' He shaded his eyes and stood on tiptoe to look across the top of the vegetation.

From the primeval world of the lounge room they walked into the world of the future. In the kitchen all was steel and light. Amelia opened the door of the eye-level, built-in oven.

'Plenty of room in there,' she said.

'Enough for an ox,' Stuart said but Amelia didn't answer. She peered at the instructions and buttons at the side of the oven. 'There's everything you could possibly want here,' she said. 'Eight.' She looked again. 'No, nine different settings. It's self-cleaning and there's a fan extractor.'

'You wouldn't know you were cooking smelly old food at all,'

Stuart said but Amelia was opening and closing all the doors near the sink.

'Plenty of cupboard space.'

'That's important.'

'It is important, Stuart,' Amelia insisted.

Stuart looked at all the multicoloured buttons, lights and switches surrounding him.

'A garbage disposal unit,' Amelia tapped an ugly looking contraption on top of the sink. Stuart watched her stroke the coppered chimney above the hotplates and stare into the microwave door at her own dark reflection. He saw her living in a world of elegance and comfort with meals cooked and hot in an instant, with fresh fruit for breakfast, where her friends came to dinner and admired her home and drank their wine from crystal glasses, where the children played quietly in the garden and baby slept safe in his cot, where dust never settled and all the smells, grease, skins, pips and bones were taken away by fans and garbage disposal units.

'After we're married,' Amelia said, 'and we have our own home, this is the sort of kitchen I want.'

'And you shall have it,' Stuart said.

Amelia smiled. 'Let's go and look at the bedroom.'

Stuart couldn't say when he first heard 'after we're married'. Over a year ago; in bed probably, lazy and relaxed on a Saturday afternoon. It would have been a natural thing to say. He might even have said it himself, but once it was said it set in motion a strange machine. A flat-car at first, rolling down a gentle gradient with only him and Amelia on board. Now it had grown into a full railway carriage hauled by a powerful diesel engine. There were seats for everyone: parents, brothers, sisters, uncles, aunts, friends and people he didn't even know — insurance salesmen, bank managers, show-home representatives — all hurtling towards the wedding day. A few months ago he would have let the flat-car roll on for ever. Now, with all these people crowding into the carriage, pushing them together on the same seat, he felt like inching away from Amelia, staring ahead and straightening his trouser leg so it didn't touch her skirt.

Amelia in one of the bedrooms called out, 'Oh Stuart! It's perfect!'

Stuart flushed. He stepped to one side and shrugged apologetically as another young couple came out through the doorway. She was in the centre of the room looking at a lace-canopied cot in one corner. The walls twittered and scampered with birds and bunny rabbits.

'I wish we were married right now,' Amelia said as Stuart put his arm around her. 'I wish we didn't have to wait so long.'

'It's only a few weeks.'

'I know, but I wish we could forget about everyone and get married right now.'

'I wish we could forget about everyone too,' said Stuart.

Amelia turned and gave him a quick kiss on the cheek. 'But we can't really, can we?'

'No, I don't suppose so.'

The corners of her mouth turned down but she lifted them into a laugh.

'The bedroom,' she said. 'That should cheer you up.'

'I wasn't depressed,' Stuart protested.

'No, not depressed.' Amelia walked ahead but said over her shoulder, 'A bit fidgety, though.' She gave the nursery a last glance. 'There's time enough to worry about babies after we're married.'

Stuart wasn't thinking of babies. He followed Amelia into the bedroom. Flowers and autumn colours was the theme, the walls covered in daisies, the bed with fallen leaves. He went over to the bed and pushed at the mattress with his hand.

'At least it doesn't squeak.'

Amelia lowered her eyelids.

'Don't,' she said. 'Someone might see.'

The tight-haired representative pursed her lips and looked at Stuart from the doorway. When she turned her back to welcome another young couple into the bedroom, Stuart poked his tongue out at her.

'Stuart,' Amelia hissed.

'This is our master bedroom,' the representative announced. The young couple looked around, wide-eyed.

'Autumn leaves in a bedroom,' Stuart said to Amelia as they left the room. 'Symbols of old age and decay.'

'The warm restful colours of autumn,' the representative said in a loud voice.

Amelia stopped outside the doorway. 'Stuart,' she said. 'Stop it. It's embarrassing.'

'Well,' he shrugged. 'She deserves it.'

The corners of Amelia's mouth went down again.

'Stuart,' she said quietly. 'Don't.'

'Don't what?'

'You know.'

He raised his voice. 'I don't know.'

'Don't spoil everything.'

'I wasn't,' Stuart said, but left it at that. Amelia was right. He wanted to spoil everything, to jump off the train, to let them go on without him, to tell her he didn't want to get married, but it was too late.

At the bottom of the stairs he stopped by a pot plant stand and tapped at a piece of veneer curling off at its edge. Amelia gave a quick look around.

'Don't do that,' she said. 'You'll damage it.'

'It's already damaged. The whole thing's coming unglued.'

'You mean we are.' Amelia turned her face from him. Her voice was so soft he thought he might not have heard her.

'What?'

She said in the same voice, 'It's not that stupid table, it's us.'

He tried to gather his thoughts; they were flying out and betraying him.

'We're coming unglued,' Amelia repeated. 'That's what you meant.'

The train stopped. Stuart tensed to prevent himself from being thrown forward. The passengers were in disarray, suitcases and aged relatives all in a heap on the floor, everyone talking and shouting together. Amelia alone sat still on the seat beside him.

'I'd like to leave now,' she said.

Outside, she cleared the dead leaves from a bench under the birch tree and sat down. Stuart sat next to her.

'I'm sorry,' he said.

Amelia tightened her lips and closed her eyes. Stuart leaned forward slightly and tried to look closer at her face. She was a long way from him. Nothing showed on her features to tell him what she thought or felt. She opened her eyes and he turned away.

'I know what's the matter,' she said.

He said nothing.

'I've known it for weeks now. I've tried not to think about it but it's no use.'

'What's no use?' Stuart noticed a wisp of hair caught in her eyelid and started to put out his hand to brush it away but thought better of it. Amelia sighed.

'Don't tell me you don't know.'

'Know what?'

She squeezed her hands into fists.

'What are you on about?' he asked, madly rehearsing in his mind what to say if she accused him of not caring for her, of not loving her, of not wanting to get married.

'You don't want to get married. Do you?' Amelia unclenched her fists and dropped her shoulders. Stuart wanted to move closer to her on the bench but she stopped him.

'Do you?' she insisted.

It would have been easy to say 'No' half an hour ago when she hadn't asked him, when she was rattling about in the kitchen, clucking in the nursery and dragging him around the show home as if he was some cumbersome but necessary instrument for the fulfilment of her dreams. Now when her dreams had fallen and lay strewn about her feet he wanted to pick them up and give them back to her.

'I don't know,' he said.

A film of tears blurred Amelia's pupils. 'I want us to be happy. That's all I've ever wanted.' She flicked a finger at the corner of each eye and straightened her shoulders. At the side of the track Stuart watched and waited to see if she would leave him there.

'If you're not going to talk,' Amelia said, 'I will.' She lifted her head.

'I'd give it all up, all of it.' She waited. Stuart couldn't think of anything to say. He watched her defiance take over.

'I don't want a lovely home,' she said. 'I don't want a smell-proof kitchen and a lacy cot. I don't.' She swallowed, and rubbed at her eyes.

'I don't want a white wedding with flowers and all those people I don't even know. I don't want any of it.'

'It's all right,' Stuart said.

'It's not all right.' Amelia lowered her head. 'It's not like it used to be.'

Stuart moved closer to her on the bench.

'It's all right,' he said and put his arm around her. 'Don't worry.'

In the background he heard a sound like a powerful diesel engine starting up.

DISTORTIONS

1

MICHAEL HAD BEEN ill. His illness from start to finish had lasted about four months. It was consumption, pulmonary tuberculosis, phthisis. He'd read the books and knew the symptoms. Not that he had many symptoms; night sweats and weight loss were the only obvious ones. He didn't even have much of a cough, and there wasn't a sign anywhere of haemorrhage. The truth was that during the time he was ill Michael never felt physically ill. Sometimes he wondered if he really was ill.

'Oh you're ill all right,' the doctor told him and showed him the shadows on his lungs. The shadows looked more like bright spots, but Michael knew from reading that shadows looked like that on X-rays. It seemed odd, all the same, to call them shadows. 'You probably developed the condition in India,' the doctor told him, and Michael could well believe this. India was full of shadows. 'In the old days,' the doctor said, 'there wasn't much we could do. Of course that didn't stop us trying just about everything, but nothing really worked. In the end the disease always won. Things are different now though.' He gave a smile of triumph. 'We've got pills for everything today.'

On the day Michael left hospital the doctor warned him against travelling in the 'exotic east' again. 'All that dirt and disease,' he said, 'it gets into everything.' Michael took his advice and decided to stay in New Zealand. The doctor was right; the dirt and disease did get into everything. If you weren't careful, it could even get into the mind and set up a dangerous fascination there, filling it so full of shadows that you'd never see the light again. There wasn't much chance of that happening in clean and scrubbed New Zealand — which, when Michael thought about it, was one of the reasons he'd gone travelling in the first place. Now, with his mind as clear as his lungs, he felt free of such dangerous ideas. He would find somewhere to live in Auckland, get a part-time job and resume his studies.

The doctor seemed pleased with Michael's plans and, though he wasn't much older than Michael, nodded his paternal approval. 'A new life,' he said, 'that's the answer,' and he was right again.

Standing on the hospital steps, with a cold and brilliant winter day all around and the air clean and fresh in his fully repaired lungs, Michael felt so healthy he hit his chest with his fists. He spent the rest of the day wandering the city streets and parks, breathing in and breathing out and enjoying every second of it. When he stayed at the youth hostel in Princes Street that night, he felt sure people were looking at him as if he were a little mad. Perhaps he was, if it was mad to be cheerful and optimistic and have a smile on your face. He was certain that everything was going to be all right, that things were going to happen just the way he wanted. Tomorrow he would find somewhere to stay and the next day a part-time job, or the day after: there was no hurry. He still had enough money to last a few weeks. He felt so positive about the future, it was all he could do to restrain himself from trying to cheer everyone up. His fellow guests at the hostel were a miserable-looking lot — staring at the playing cards in their hands as if they were death warrants, or rummaging through their back packs as if they were searching for dead rodents. One guest in Hitler Jugend shorts was sitting bent over the edge of his bunk with a pen in his hand composing a suicide note, while the woman with him ate pickled cockroaches from an opened tin can on her lap. The answer to all their problems was somewhere in Michael's head, and if he could only put it into words, it would cheer them up instantly and permanently.

One of the card players looked up from his hand and frowned. Michael wanted to take him by the arm and drag him outside to show him what a bright and shiny world they lived in. The card player looked across at him and frowned even more.

Michael decided his fellow guests were in no mood to be cheered up. In fact he was beginning to find them vaguely irritating, which didn't suit him one bit. He jumped up suddenly and went out into Princes Street. The street lights came on one after the other as he walked up to the university. He had the odd idea that someone in a high city building was watching him and had switched on the lights especially for his benefit.

At the student café he bought a pink-iced cake with a cherry on top and a plastic cup of tea-bag tea. He ate the cake in a single mouthful and drank the tea straight down. They were both delicious. There was a copy of the student newspaper opened out on the bench next to him. Someone had spilt tomato sauce on the middle of the page, but Michael read it all the same — an article about the poor polluted world being slowly choked, corroded, hacked and poisoned to death. Michael didn't believe a word of it and laughed quietly to himself, but not quietly enough to avoid being overheard by the girl at the opposite end of the table. She was as thin and pale and beautiful as all the other thin and pale and beautiful girls at university. Michael had a strange neurotic affair with her. She was vague and dreamy and subject to fits of melancholy. Michael loved her very much but was never able to cheer her up. The whole affair was over very quickly — in as much time as it takes someone to look at you and look away.

'Do you think the world's doomed?' Michael asked, but the girl turned the page in her book and didn't answer. 'Well I don't,' said Michael, and bought another cherry-topped cake on his way out. As he walked back to the hostel, he knew for certain that good news awaited him. It wasn't easy to find. Most of the kill-joy club were asleep or reading books about *angst* and *weltschmerz*. The man at the desk, wearing shorts in the middle of winter, with fine golden hairs on his suntanned mountaineer's arms and legs, had no idea what Michael was talking about.

'I haven't got any news for you,' he said, shaking his head. Michael could see that the mountaineer had never had a day sick in his life and probably never would. He was far too healthy in body and mind to ever have TB or intuitions.

'I was expecting something,' said Michael, without a trace of disappointment. He knew for certain that good news was very close by.

'Nothing here,' said the mountaineer, but he was wrong. Over his left shoulder, on the notice board, was the good news Michael had been waiting for. A small white card was pinned up with a single drawing pin and half covered by the edge of a Save Our Forests poster. Michael went around the side of the desk for a closer look. The white card was yellowing around the edges and the corners were curled in. He lifted the bottom of the poster and read the good news on the card. It was written in fountain pen, and the black ink was faded and rusting.

ACCOMMODATION
PERMANENT AND CASUAL
GOOD RATES
KALAZIAN'S BOARDING HOUSE
27 KINGSLAND TERRACE
KINGSLAND
PHONE 860545

It was perfect. Michael borrowed a pen from the mountaineer and copied down the address and phone number. He wondered if he should take down the card and throw it away so no one could steal the boarding house from him. As quick as he thought this, though, he laughed at the idea. Now he had found it, he knew it was his. He took more than an hour to go to sleep that night, he was so excited.

Mr Edward Kalazian was not in charge of Kalazian's Boarding House; he only behaved as if he was. His wife, Mrs Edward Kalazian, was the true proprietor, Mr Kalazian explained. 'To clear up any misunderstandings; not that we anticipate any misunderstandings,' he was quick to add.

Kalazian's was, as Michael knew it would be, perfect. It was a kauri mansion fallen on hard times; big and old and full of narrow stairways and corridors. There were doors everywhere;

alongside the corridors, under the stairs, in the floors and ceilings. He itched to find out what was behind them. The stairs creaked like stairs ought, as Mr Kalazian led the way. Michael knew he was going to be very happy at Kalazian's. The pictures on the wall at the side of the stairs were evidence of that; Victorian prints of Benares, the Red Fort at Agra and the deserted city of Fatehpur Sikri. At the top of the stairs, to add to his pleasure, above a print of the Himalayas was a kukri. Its leather scabbard was old and cracked and the bindings on the handle frayed where the fingers had gripped it.

'This place,' said Mr Kalazian without turning around, 'is a museum,' but he wasn't apologising. 'We,' he laughed, 'that is, Mrs Kalazian and I, pride ourselves on its lack of modern amenities.' It was hardly the standard patter for someone hoping to impress a prospective tenant, but perhaps Mr Kalazian knew exactly what he was doing. Michael was even more pleased. The truth was that Mr Kalazian had already impressed him. His physical size would have been enough to impress anyone. He was large enough to fill a doorway, with beard and eyes to match, but more than this there was a perversity about him which immediately appealed to Michael. He felt sure his relationship with Mr Kalazian would mature or degenerate into something other than that of mere landlord and tenant.

The mid-morning sun in a clear winter sky shone straight through a tall window at the end of the corridor and picked out the dust dancing around Mr Kalazian's shoulder as he opened the door to Michael's room. Michael knew before he even saw it that the room would be perfect too. It was small, but the window looking out to the jumbled houses of Grey Lynn and Newton was so large it made the room seem twice its real size. The floor was bare apart from a small carpet at the front of the bed. The bed itself and other furniture, what little there was — a wardrobe with a mirror on its door, a bedside locker, two spindly chairs and a small table in front of the window — were all dark oak, not a trace of chrome, formica or plastic anywhere.

'It's perfect,' Michael said and swung his pack off his back and on to the floor.

'I knew you'd like it,' Mr Kalazian beamed. 'I could tell at a glance when I first saw you. The table,' he said walking across and patting it, 'can of course serve as a desk. No bookcase, I'm afraid, but not to worry.' He caught sight of his reflection in the mirror and smoothed down the front of his black pullover by way of caressing himself. He obviously thought he was a fine figure of a man and Michael agreed.

'I'm sure I have one somewhere you can use,' Mr Kalazian said.

'Sorry?' said Michael, forgetting what Mr Kalazian had been talking about.

'A bookcase,' Mr Kalazian laughed.

'Yes,' Michael returned his laugh, 'I suppose I'll need one.'

'Suppose?' Mr Kalazian frowned in mock disapproval. 'There's no suppose about it. A student must have a desk and a bookcase otherwise, well, there's no telling what might happen. The whole fabric of the universe might come unravelled.' He lowered his voice conspiratorially. 'Mrs Kalazian,' he said, 'is suspicious of you.' Michael blinked and was about to ask why but Mr Kalazian explained. 'Being a student and all,' he said, 'and having no family to speak of, she wonders, such is the concern of women with wordly matters, how you will pay the rent.' He pulled out one of the spindly chairs and sat in it to ponder Michael.

'She didn't say anything,' Michael said.

'Ah, no. She wouldn't,' Kalazian tapped the top of the table with his finely manicured fingernails. 'But I know her,' he said. 'She'll be wondering; you can rely on it.'

'I've got enough to last a few weeks,' Michael began but Mr Kalazian stopped him with a raised hand.

'I know what I'll do,' he said. 'I'll tell her a lie. It's one of the things I love to do.'

'Why not tell her the truth?' asked Michael, but Mr Kalazian wouldn't hear of it.

'No, no,' he dismissed the idea with a wave. 'A lie is by far the best thing. It's good exercise for the brain.'

It also had the advantage of creating a bond between him and Kalazian, Michael thought.

'Besides,' Mr Kalazian went on, 'I can see we are to be friends and there's nothing like a shared lie to improve a friendship, don't you agree?'

'Yes,' said Michael and was about to take out the other chair when Kalazian stood up and smoothed down his pullover again. 'Good, that's settled,' he said. 'You can bring down the rent when you're ready.' He looked as if he had finished his business and was about to leave before Michael had time to collect his thoughts. 'It's better you don't know the lie,' Mr Kalazian anticipated him. 'All you have to do is act normally. She won't suspect a thing.'

Michael wasn't as practised in lying as Mr Kalazian obviously was and wondered if, after all, deceiving his landlady was such a good idea. He didn't object to the deception on moral grounds but he was worried in case he did or said something that would expose him and Mr Kalazian; especially Mr Kalazian, who had been so kind.

'What if I do or say something?' he said, but again Mr Kalazian was ready for him.

'You won't,' he said. 'Nothing you could do or say would expose the lie; not even the truth.' He smiled benignly. 'You must learn to trust me, Michael,' he said. 'Believe me, I'm very good at this sort of thing.'

'I do trust you,' said Michael, then added, 'to be a good liar.' They both laughed and Mrs Kalazian's voice came up the stairs, wavered along the corridor and crept in faintly through the half-open door.

'Edward,' it said.

Mr Kalazian crossed himself. 'Coming, my dear,' he called and followed the voice obediently down the stairs.

That night Michael had difficulty getting off to sleep. He decided it was because he was still excited about how well things had gone. Mr Kalazian had been as good as his word. When Michael returned from buying sandwiches for lunch there was a bookcase next to his desk; dark oak to match the other furniture. There was a note on it and Michael recognised the hand as the same one that had written the card at the youth hostel. 'No extra charge,' it said and was signed, 'Edward K.'

Mr Kalazian was with his wife, eating soup in the downstairs kitchen. 'Glad to help, glad to help,' he said when Michael thanked him. Even Mrs Kalazian seemed pleased and between mouthfuls of soup managed a quick smile. Whatever lie Mr Kalazian had told her seemed to be working.

In the evening when Michael came back from the Chinese take-away with a celebratory nasi goreng as hot as they could make it, Mr Kalazian stopped him at the bottom of the stairs.

'Michael,' he said and stroked the polished wooden knob of the banister. 'Have you thought about a job?'

For a second Michael thought Mrs Kalazian had been wondering about the rent again but Mr Kalazian was quick to reasssure him.

'I know you said you had enough money for a few weeks and we, that is Mrs Kalazian and I, are not worried in the least about your ability to pay the rent.' He leant closer to Michael and his breath smelt of fried kidneys and rum. 'It's just that if you should want a job I might, indeed will, be able to help you.'

Michael had become so used to everything going right he wasn't surprised. In fact he had expected this to happen.

'That'd be great,' he enthused.

Mr Kalazian grinned. 'Good,' he said, then raising his voice, 'I'll see you in the morning about it.' He breathed in noisily through his nose. 'Nasi goreng,' he sighed. 'Hot as they can make it.'

'You can have some if you like.' Michael hoped Mr Kalazian wouldn't take him up on the offer. Mr Kalazian smiled and nodded to tease him then said, 'No thanks,' and waved Michael up the stairs.

Given all that had happened, Michael had every reason to be excited; it was no wonder he had difficulty getting off to sleep. He had almost convinced himself this was the reason for his insomnia when the full moon shining through the window on the back of his neck told him it wasn't. The notion that everything might not be all right came to him. He pulled the bedclothes over his head but the idea wouldn't go away.

He had to laugh when he finally worked out what was happening. He was tired. It was late at night and he was about to go to sleep. All the superstitions and irrational ideas which he hadn't acknowledged or entertained for days had seized the opportunity while his guard was relaxed to come out and give themselves an airing in the moonlight. Well, there was no harm in allowing them a little exercise — keeping them cooped up would be more dangerous; they would only seethe and sulk and plot against him. They could nip and snarl and skulk about looking for something to pounce on if they wanted, but they wouldn't find anything. Everything was going to be all right and there was no evidence anywhere for them to try and prove otherwise.

He turned over and stared his defiance at the moon. Someone was coughing downstairs and a door clicked shut. The moon had climbed almost beyond the corner of the window but its light threw the shadow of a bent cross against the floor and wall beside his bed. He clenched his fists and flung off the bedclothes. The scampering little superstitions had had more than enough exercise for one day. The floorboards were cold against his bare feet and creaked as he walked across to the window.

In a last effort to unsettle him someone, a woman, was weeping quietly to herself in the room next to his. He'd been in his room all evening and hadn't heard anyone come up the stairs or go in next door. The scalp behind his ears tingled at the thought that while he had been so happy, so full of optimism and certainty, relishing every forkful of nasi goreng, someone only the thickness of a wall away had been so quiet and sad. He sighed angrily. Enough was enough. The curtains screeched and hissed as he dragged them together at the centre of the window and shut out the moon completely. He went over to the wall and put his ear against it. The weeping, if indeed there had been any, had stopped.

2

Her name was Anna; at least that's what the towel across her arm had printed on it. She wore another towel wrapped in a turban around her head and a long blue dressing gown with golden Chinese characters on one lapel. Although the corridor was easily wide enough to allow two or even three people to pass comfortably, Michael stood to one side as she closed the bathroom door behind her.

Her eyes were slightly bloodshot and red-rimmed, but that might have been from the shower. 'Thanks,' she said and smiled without a trace of embarrassment.

She was different from the woman Michael had imagined weeping in the room next to his, young, thin, nervous, pale and sensitive. Anna had faint lines at the corners of her mouth and eyes and her shoulders and hips were too wide for the waif of Michael's imagination. She smelled so warm that he closed his eyes and fell in love with her as she left him standing at the bathroom door. She probably wasn't from the room next to his where the real waif lived and was yet to emerge. He pretended to check his soap container for soap before entering the bathroom but then quickly looked over his shoulder to see where she had gone. She opened the door next to his room, turned her head and smiled at him again as she went inside.

When Michael pulled the shower curtain closed he found a long dark hair on the back of it. It squeaked when he ran it between his thumb and forefinger and curled up tight when he let it go. If he kept it, he might, with the help of magic, cast a spell on Anna, the same spell that she had cast on him. He wondered, as the hair disappeared down the plughole, why Anna, so confident as to smile at him twice, would sob to herself in the night. One day when their love affair had reached the point where they could share confidences, as Michael was sure it would, he would ask her. Halfway through his lovemaking the shower started to run cold. He turned it off. Someone knocked at the door and tried the handle. He was about to say something when a man's voice whispered hoarsely through the keyhole. 'It's only me. Why have you locked the door?'

Michael coughed deeply. 'I won't be long,' he called and jealousy seeped into him like bile. He dried himself quickly and put his dressing gown on but he knew as he picked up the soap container that his rival had gone. When he opened the door there was no one outside but he heard a door close on the floor above him. It hadn't taken Michael that long to dry himself; his rival must have been very quick to get up the stairs in such a short time. Unless Anna was attracted to sneaky little cowards, which given her hips and shoulders was not likely, Michael need fear nothing from the competition.

'The man,' Mr Kalazian informed Michael over a breakfast of steaming porridge, 'is a homosexual.'

Michael was amazed at Mr Kalazian's ability to eat large spoonfuls of porridge without any of it sticking to his beard and moustache.

'Not,' Mr Kalazian continued, 'that either I or Mrs Kalazian condemn Mr Charles's sexual preferences. We are both quite broadminded in that respect.' Mrs Kalazian, standing behind her husband, raised her eyes and snorted.

Mr Kalazian shook another teaspoon of brown sugar on to his porridge and waited for it to melt. 'It's his sneakiness we object to,' he said. 'Furtively smuggling young boys up to his room as if it were some shameful sin. Sodomy, I'm sure you as an educated man would agree, is no crime. Sneakiness on the other hand is. A paltry one at that,' he added.

'He's a good tenant.' Mrs Kalazian widened her eyes briefly at Michael and the kettle whistled in agreement.

Mr Kalazian paid no attention to either his wife or the kettle. 'If Mr Charles fancies himself a sinner,' he said, 'he'll have to do better than sodomy. There are far worse things than that. It hardly warrants the destruction of entire cities any more. Not,' he mumbled through a mouthful of porridge, 'that it ever did.'

Mrs Kalazian put a mug of tea beside the porridge bowl. 'He pays the rent,' she said.

'Indeed he does,' Mr Kalazian slurped a mouthful of tea. 'Which brings us to the point.'

Michael straightened up in his chair as with his head bent and eyes closed Mr Kalazian came to the point.

'A job,' he said with his head still bent. 'I promised I would do something for you.' He tapped the centre of his forehead with his middle finger, blinked his eyes and stared directly at the bridge of Michael's nose. 'Disconcerting, isn't it?'

Michael couldn't focus his eyes on Mr Kalazian's and knew that he was playing some vaguely sadistic game with him. He liked Mr Kalazian all the more. 'What,' he said, 'the job?'

Mr Kalazian laughed. 'No, staring at the bridge of your nose. It makes it difficult for you to focus your eyes on mine.'

Michael laughed with him. 'It's as if your eyes were looking right through me,' he said. 'It's *very* disconcerting.'

'Yes,' said Mr Kalazian. 'I do it to Mr Charles all the time. It makes him squirm and stutter. I'm sure he thinks I'm looking into his soul.' He swallowed the last spoonful of porridge and patted his pullovered belly with satisfaction. 'He can't see through the trick like you.'

Michael was pleased. He had passed Mr Kalazian's first test and was ready for the next.

'Now,' Mr Kalazian went on in a serious tone, looking Michael straight in the eye this time. Mrs Kalazian leaned against the corner of the draining board behind her husband and warmed her hands around a cup of tea. Michael was disappointed he hadn't been offered one but Mr Kalazian didn't allow him to sulk.

'You're a student,' he said, and though it wasn't a question, Michael answered, 'Yes.'

'What is it you study?' asked Mr Kalazian as his wife eyed Michael across the rim of her cup.

'Philosophy and psychology.'

Mr Kalazian's eyes widened. 'Dangerous subjects for a

sensitive mind.' Michael was flattered to think he thought him sensitive.

'And not immediately apparent to the uneducated mind as having any association with financial reward.'

'No,' Michael admitted and wondered why, if Mr Kalazian and his wife had no worries about his ability to pay the rent, they were both harping on about money.

In his uncanny way Mr Kalazian once more anticipated Michael. 'You think,' he said, 'that Mrs Kalazian and I are inordinately concerned with money?'

Michael knew Mr Kalazian had the power to read his thoughts but before he could stop himself blurted out, 'No, not at all,' and felt himself blush.

Mr Kalazian laughed. 'You're not a very good liar. The fact is Mrs Kalazian and I are concerned with money, not, I hasten to add,' he hastened to add, 'inordinately concerned, but concerned nonetheless.'

Mrs Kalazian closed her eyes and sighed. 'The point,' she said with her teeth clenched.

Mr Kalazian shook his head. 'Mrs Kalazian,' he whispered loudly, 'has no taste for circumlocution but as usual she's right.' He gripped his chair at the sides, pushed himself away from the table and brought both hands down on his knees with a loud slap. 'How would you like to manage a small bookshop,' he said, 'on Ponsonby Road, catering for exclusive and eccentric tastes, two hundred dollars a week, starting tomorrow, no questions asked?'

'No questions asked?' It was an odd phrase and Michael frowned.

'That's a question,' said Mr Kalazian.

'Sorry,' Michael hastened. 'It's very kind of you.'

Mrs Kalazian took away her husband's porridge bowl and mug. 'But would you like it?' Mr Kalazian asked.

'Yes,' Michael said, then for emphasis, 'Yes, I would.' He started to itch and burn with questions. Two hundred dollars a week was very generous when Mr Kalazian knew a full-time job was not part of Michael's plans. Exclusive and eccentric tastes had a dangerous ring to it and 'no questions asked' made the whole thing even more intriguing.

'I know,' said Mr Kalazian, 'that a man with an inquisitive mind and a taste for the bizarre, which any student of philosophy and psychology must have, would now be itching and burning with questions.' He stood up and gestured to Michael to do the same.

'Yes, I am,' Michael admitted, hoping Mr Kalazian might at least allow him a few, but Mr Kalazian put his arm around Michael's shoulder and walked him towards the door. He had the repellently seductive smell of a warm rug.

'Your strength,' said Mr Kalazian, 'is in your pursuit of the truth. I can see that and believe me,' he smiled with narrowed eyes, 'I admire it, but such an ideal presents us with a paradox.'

Michael nodded to keep him talking. 'A paradox,' he said eagerly.

Mr Kalazian walked with him along the corridor to the foot of the stairs and stopped.

'The pursuit of truth,' he said, 'by its very nature is best carried out by the naïve. Cynics such as myself know that the truth is unattainable.' Full of enthusiasm for the argument, Michael was about to counter this idea but Mr Kalazian held up his hand to stop him.

'The naïve,' he said, 'by their optimism and persistence sometimes discover what they believe to be the truth and then proceed to tell everyone. They believe "the truth will set you free", whereas the cynic believes no such thing. He knows the truth is best kept secret. The naïve discover the truth but don't know how to deal with it; the cynic knows how to deal with it but never discovers it. There's the paradox,' he said and laughed.

Michael had travelled the globe or half of it, and one of his intentions had been to become a man of the world. He hadn't succeeded. A man of the world would never have developed consumption or so easily have fallen in love. 'You're right,' he said.

'Of course I am.' Mr Kalazian caressed the knob on the

banister. 'But I admire you nonetheless. You will discover the truth one day; I'm sure of it. A man with your mind could not help but do so. In the meantime though,' he took his hand from the banister as the top of the stairs creaked behind Michael, 'leave the truth with me. It's safer that way.'

Anna, smelling so sweet the tips of Michael's fingers tingled, brushed past him as she came down the stairs. She gave him a sidelong glance then flashed a smile at Mr Kalazian.

'Morning, Eddie,' she said. She looked younger with her hair down and on the right lapel of her jacket was a small brooch fashioned of leather in the form of a flower.

'Anna, meet Michael.' Mr Kalazian patted a proprietorial hand on Michael's back.

Anna shook his hand. 'Hello, Michael,' she smiled as if they shared some secret Mr Kalazian knew nothing about. He madly tried to think of something to say that would impress her with his originality and intelligence and the fact that he had seen the dark side of India and recently recovered from a romantic illness. 'Pleased to meet you,' he managed but before he could think of anything else she was halfway down the outside steps with the front door closed behind her.

Mr Kalazian's voice cut through his reverie. 'Mrs Kalazian,' he said, 'is of the opinion that Miss Jankovich, that is, Anna, is in her own way as much a deviant as Mr Charles. What do you think?' he asked as if the question was on an obscure point of philosophy.

Michael thought Mrs Kalazian was right. There was something deviant about Anna, but then the same could be said of anyone.

'I suppose she's right,' he said, 'if it's deviant to be smiling and friendly.'

'Precisely what I told her,' Mr Kalazian was stroking his throat. 'But Mrs Kalazian like all women is very perceptive of other women.'

He was about to leave Michael with the thought when the bathroom door upstairs slammed and someone stamped along the corridor. Mr Kalazian hunched his shoulders. 'Mallis,' he whispered and tiptoed to his kitchen to leave Michael with that thought instead.

At the end of another day when Michael had managed to convince himself that everything had gone right apart from Mrs Kalazian's opinion of Anna and Mallis, whoever or whatever that was, Mrs Kalazian ambushed him inside the front door when he came back from the university library. He was in a hurry to get to his room and bury himself in his books. His illness had put him behind in his studies and there was a lot to catch up on. Mrs Kalazian, her arms folded and a feather duster in one hand as a symbol of her authority, greeted him with an unpleasant smile.

'We've had a complaint,' she said.

For a second — it couldn't have been longer — Michael had the irrational urge to snatch the feather duster off Mrs Kalazian and hit her over the head with it. He recovered himself and said as any innocent person would say, 'Oh.'

'From Mr Mallis.'

Aptly named, thought Michael, but attempted a pleasant smile. Mrs Kalazian wasn't having it.

'He's a valued tenant,' she went on, 'and I won't have him upset. We've been more than kind to you I think, especially Edward, and this sort of unpleasantness is very upsetting.' She unfolded her arms and put her hands on her hips as if she expected an explanation. Michael felt despair slithering about in his stomach and swallowed to keep it down.

If he wasn't careful, his good humour and optimism would disappear and his mind, as fresh and clean as his lungs, would be full of demons and dirt again. Through the open kitchen door at the end of the corridor he caught sight of Kalazian, who gave him a breezy wave. He tried a half wave in reply and a nod over Mrs Kalazian's shoulder. She sighed noisily through her nose.

'I'm sorry,' Michael said and coughed to give himself time to collect his thoughts. 'What exactly is Mr Mallis complaining about?'

'Exactly' was the wrong word. Michael knew it before it was

through his lips. Mrs Kalazian caught it and threw it back at him.

'Exactly this,' she said. 'Mr Mallis says you wrote his name on the steamed-up bathroom mirror.'

'What?' Michael said though he heard her perfectly well.

'I think you heard me perfectly well.'

All the rage and pleasure of the victim of injustice bubbled up inside him and was about to boil over when Mr Kalazian opened the kitchen door wide and shook his head with a finger to his lips. Evidently satisifed that Michael had taken the complaint quietly, Mrs Kalazian softened her tone.

'Look,' she said. 'I know you've got your problems.'

Problems? What problems? Again Mr Kalazian stopped Michael with a wince and a gesture.

'We've all got our problems,' Mrs Kalazian continued, 'but it's a rule in this house that we don't take them out on other people.'

'And a very wise rule too.' Kalazian joined his wife as if he had just strolled out of the kitchen and caught the tail-end of her dissertation. 'Wouldn't you agree, Michael?'

'Yes, I would.' With Kalazian's eyes on him he didn't add that Mr Mallis should stick to that rule.

'Then we'll say no more about it.' Mrs Kalazian gave a single nod to show that the conversation was at an end. 'I hope you know what you're doing,' she added to her husband then turned and opened the door next to her. Michael just had time to see a fireplace with a large mirror above it and a highly polished rosewood china cabinet full of delicate cups and fragile plates never meant to be used, then the key turned in the lock behind her.

'She'll be lost in there for hours now. Listen.' Kalazian inclined his head towards the door. Michael held his breath and heard the muffled sound of heavy curtains being drawn.

'To keep the world out,' said Kalazian, 'while she sits on the sofa with a glass of sherry in her hand and cries.'

Michael was finding it more and more difficult to maintain the euphoria that had been with him since he left hospital. If it was to be continually tested like this it wouldn't be long before he'd be drawing the curtains too. For all that Michael liked him, Kalazian wasn't helping either with his shaking of the head and fingers to the lips business. 'If you'd let me tell the truth,' he said, 'there'd be no need for tears.'

Kalazian tutted loudly and frowned. Michael remembered his lesson on truth and felt like apologising for the poor student that he was. 'Don't apologise,' Kalazian said. 'There's no harm done. Mrs Kalazian will have put this unpleasantness behind her by tomorrow and we can continue as if nothing had happened.'

In spite of his lesson, Michael couldn't resist saying, 'I didn't write Mallis's name on the mirror.'

Kalazian put his hand to his mouth and stifled a laugh. 'As if you would,' he spluttered. 'As if you would.'

'Then you believe me?' Michael suddenly wanted to make a full confession, to tell Kalazian everything and receive his absolution. He grabbed hold of the idea and stuffed it back in his head before it turned round and swallowed him.

'Of course I believe you.' Kalazian examined his shiny fingernails with a critical eye. 'But enough of this. Let us, as Mrs Kalazian puts it, say no more about it.'

Michael wanted to say a lot more about it. He had been wrongfully accused. There was a buckle in the otherwise smooth track leading into the future and he wanted it straightened out. But like an avuncular and overfed archbishop, Kalazian raised his hand and gave Michael his blessing along with a prophecy.

'Blessed are they who hunger and thirst after justice,' he said. 'For one day they'll get it and then God help us all.' He patted Michael's shoulder. 'The buckle in the track,' he said, 'only sways the carriage a little. Don't worry; it won't derail you.' He headed back to the kitchen and after all his deep-voiced wisdom, without turning his head, said cheerily as if he had just finished talking about the weather, 'I'll see you tomorrow about the bookshop. Seven-thirty all right?'

'Fine,' said Michael and with his books in his pack started up the stairs where he was almost elbowed to one side by a tighttrousered, short-haired man with blue eyes full of tears. Mr Charles for sure.

'I'm sorry, sorry,' Mr Charles sniffled and glanced quickly at Michael as he ran past him up the stairs. He held a handkerchief to his nose and the front of his white shirt and the sleeve of his pale grey windcheater were spattered with blood. When he was out of sight along the first floor corridor, Michael heard a contemptuous laugh which without a doubt came from Mallis. He took the stairs two at a time and rehearsed in his head the confrontation to come, something along the lines of, 'If you have any complaints about me I'd like you to see me first; it's only fair.' Nothing too aggressive, but letting Mallis know how he felt.

The kukri in its scabbard caught his eye and distracted him as a door at the end of the corridor clicked shut. Michael clenched his fists in disappointment. He placed his pack on the floor and his palms tingled. He looked quickly down the stairs. The smell of Bolognese sauce floated up to him, followed by the leathery squeak and pop of a wine cork and Kalazian singing like a drunken gondolier. His stomach felt as if it had been scoured out. His heart grew to fill his chest and hammered for release. He took the scabbard off the wall as quiet as a thief and removed the blade.

It was so smooth and glistening it looked as if it was made of mercury but it was hard and when Michael ran his thumb across its edge every ridge was picked out and caught. A floorboard creaked behind him. It was Mallis. Michael caught his breath and darted a look across his shoulder but there was nobody there. Just as well. If the misshapen Mallis had been standing there grinning and glinty-eyed like a malignant dwarf it would have only taken a second to sweep the blade around and slice off his head. With murderous thoughts like that on the loose he decided it was best to put the blade back in the scabbard but something stopped him. He'd heard somewhere, though it probably wasn't true, a myth made up to increase a schoolboy's awe of the Gurkhas as if they weren't already awesome enough, that once the blade was removed from its scabbard it had to draw blood before it was put back.

He could, in fact he should, have dismissed the idea for the superstition it was and replaced the blade straight away but knew, if he did, the superstition would nag away at him and keep him awake. He placed the scabbard back on the wall and held the palm of his left hand out in front of him. The fleshy part at the base of his thumb was as plump as a chicken leg. He ran the tip of the blade halfway along it and for two seconds it seemed nothing had happened. Then, prickling out one after the other in a straight line, tiny beads of blood appeared, joined together and ran down towards his wrist.

A floorboard creaked behind him. It was Mallis. Michael caught his breath and darted a glance across his shoulder. Mallis wasn't a misshapen dwarf. He was a head taller than Michael and although he must have been easily forty, his hair was black and smoothed flat and shiny with brilliantine. He smiled slowly without showing his teeth and said nothing. Michael hurriedly covered the cut in his palm with the fingers of the same hand while fumbling about trying to get the blade back into the scabbard. Mallis stepped forward and held the scabbard steady. His little finger was missing and the others were long and bony.

'My name's Mallis,' he hissed out of the side of his mouth and Michael almost saw his flickering tongue.

'Michael,' said Michael and with the kukri safe where it belonged held out his hand. Mallis didn't take it. His eyes were fixed on Michael's other hand where the sticky blood oozed between the fingers. Rain pattered on the corrugated iron roof a floor and an attic above; slowly at first, then it began to rattle and drum. Michael wanted to run outside and wash all the cobwebs and superstitions and blood away.

'You've cut yourself,' Mallis said and his pupils widened.

The rain drummed harder and Kalazian accompanied his singing with the clatter of pots and pans. The smile left Mallis's face. There were spiky black hairs growing out of his nostrils. Michael felt hollow inside. It was the end of everything going right. It was as if he had gone for a walk in the bush with the sun all around and suddenly, in a place he thought was safe and familiar, discovered a gathering of witches.

'Say nothing of this to anyone.' Mallis's three-fingered hand writhed at his side.

'I won't,' Michael pushed past him. 'I won't and I haven't.' Kalazian's kitchen orchestra reached a crescendo with the multiple bangings of cupboard doors.

He made it to his room and locked the door behind him. One of his windows was open. His books on the desk and the papers that hadn't blown on the floor were spattered with rainwater. He was sure he hadn't opened the window but frowned because he wasn't certain. Without thinking he closed the window with his left hand and opened up the cut on his palm. There was an almost clean handkerchief in the drawer of his bedside locker. He wrapped it around his palm, sat on his bed and all the lemon-fragranced happiness and optimism given him with his freshly laundered body three days ago finally disappeared. He lay down flat on the bed without taking his shoes off and closed his eyes. When he awoke the rain and the bleeding had stopped. He unwrapped the handkerchief and put it in his pocket. He had been dreaming about something important, something that would explain what was going on and why his happiness had been taken away, but like all the important dreams he had ever had it flew away like paper up the chimney before he had time to catch it.

He was hungry. The Chinese take-away up the road did hamburgers and chips and there was quarter of an hour to spare before it closed. Michael sneaked out of the house so quietly the back of his neck went cold and at the Chinese take-away his happiness was restored. A little Chinese girl no more than three years old was sitting on the counter in a short cotton frock. She wore bright red polished shoes buttoned down at the side with a shiny red button. Her lacquered black hair was cut in a fringe straight across her forehead and she giggled and kicked her feet.

Anna was leaning against one of the video machines at the end of the counter and pulled a funny face at the girl, which made her giggle more. She noticed Michael and gave him a wave. 'Isn't she gorgeous?' she said.

Michael nodded while stealing a glance at Anna's eyes and the faint lines at the corners of her mouth. The woman behind the counter lifted her child onto the floor as if she was lifting a porcelain vase. The little girl frowned then grinned, running off laughing through the door at the back of the kitchen. Her mother picked up a pencil and scribble pad and smiled at Michael.

'Have the combination fried rice,' said Anna. 'I'll go you halves.'

Michael looked at her quickly but there was no need. It was all settled; he was having combination fried rice in Anna's room tonight. The woman behind the counter glanced at Anna with her pen raised and her smile unchanged.

'Combination fried rice,' Michael said.

Back in her room Anna sat Michael down on a big black cushion and poured him a glass of wine from a wine cask in her fridge.

'What do you reckon on this place?' she asked, handing him the glass.

With only a single shaded light on in the corner of the room the place seemed to be full of big black cushions, vague oriental paintings and dusty op-shop clothes thrown about on the op-shop furniture. It had a feeling of warmth about it even before the one-bar electric heater began to work.

'It's very nice,' he said and took a sip of his wine.

'Nice?' Anna looked at him in disbelief and laughed. He tried to catch sight of her eyes but they took on a dreamy look which made it hard for him to focus. He noticed she hadn't poured herself a glass of wine and wondered if she was high on something. 'You think this place is *nice*?'

He guessed she must have been talking about the house and laughed himself. 'I meant this room,' he said.

Anna spooned out the combination fried rice onto two plates. 'This room's okay, I suppose.' She looked around it quickly as if she wasn't too sure. 'But the rest of the place isn't nice.' She handed Michael one of the plates and a fork. 'It's weird. Haven't you noticed?' She pummelled the cushion next to Michael into shape and sat down on it.

'I've spent the last two days trying not to,' Michael said as she reached her arm over to the table behind her and picked up her own plate and fork. One of the weird things Michael had tried not to notice was Anna weeping to herself the other night.

'I'm not complaining.' She was poking about at her meal as if there was something alive in it. 'I like weird things.' Her eyes brightened. 'Don't you?'

'Depends how weird.' Michael was trying not to betray himself too early. The cut on his left hand started to itch. He hid his hand under his plate and wondered how he was going to explain his behaviour to Anna without sounding weird himself. She put her plate down, walked across to a cupboard above a sink in a corner of the room, opened it and took down a big plastic box. Michael took the opportunity to check his hand; it wasn't bleeding much. He felt in his pocket for his handkerchief but before he could pull it out she said, 'Give me your hand.' Without further ado she dabbed the cut with an iodine-soaked cottonwool ball and stuck six tiny strips of sticky paper along it and a sticking plaster on top.

Michael had an explanation ready but he couldn't use it. It was a lie. There hadn't been a silly accident. Anna knew everything about him. He finished his meal in silence as Anna watched him.

'Don't be angry,' she said when he put his fork down.

'I'm not,' he said and she slowly shook her head.

He smiled at her. 'Allow me a few lies,' he pleaded.

She peered at him as if there was a message on his face she couldn't make out, then laughed nervously. Michael thought whatever she was taking had started to wear off.

'Don't mind me,' she said. 'I talk nonsense sometimes.'

He could feel her escaping, running through his fingers like water.

'I'll put some music on,' she said and jumped up. 'We can lie back and listen to it and then you can go.'

'I'll go now, if you like,' Michael started to get up. She bent over the stereo, clenched her fists and gave a quick sigh.

'No,' she said. 'Listen to the music first. I want you to.'

He knew it was going to be strange hypnotic music that came in coloured ribbons winding themselves around and around until they'd wrapped him up and delivered him helpless and enchanted at her feet. It turned out to be Joe Cocker's 'Cocker Happy', badly pock-marked and not at all enchanting. Anna lay back on the cushion beside Michael and Michael held her hand to keep her from weeping. When the music finished she walked with him to the door. There were tears in her eyes but she smiled and said, 'Same again tomorrow?'

Back in his room he listened at the wall but couldn't hear anything. He was so in love he felt like doing forward rolls across the full length of the floor, so he did.

3

Michael had two pickled onions for breakfast which gave him heartburn. Kalazian with garlic on his breath and one hand on the steering wheel offered him an indigestion tablet.

'Mrs Kalazian,' he said as Michael sucked the tablet, 'awoke last night and complained that someone was rolling about in the room above us.'

'Oh,' said Michael and nearly swallowed the tablet.

'I persuaded her that she must have been dreaming.' Kalazian dabbed at the brakes as the truck in front slowed down.

'She must have been,' said Michael and the tablet stuck to the roof of his mouth.

'I haven't accused you,' said Kalazian, 'and I'm not going to. It's no crime to roll around on the floor or along its full length for that matter. Under certain circumstances it's perfectly understandable.' Michael tried to lick the tablet off the roof of his mouth with his tongue.

'If I were in a state of religious ecstasy, for instance,' Kalazian continued as they turned at the lights into Ponsonby Road, 'I might be moved to roll about on the floor. Fortunately, for a man of my bulk and for the sake of the floorboards and my marriage, I've never been in such a state.' His fingers wriggled like sexually aroused sausages. 'You're not in a state of religious ecstasy are you?' he asked and pulled over into the centre of the road to make a right-hand turn.

Michael flicked the tablet off the roof of his mouth and said, 'No.'

'Good, good.' Kalazian turned right with a flourish and parked the car at the top of Anglesea Street. He quietly pulled on the handbrake. 'Religious ecstasy might be a difficult state to maintain at the bookshop.'

Michael crunched the tablet and swallowed it. Kalazian glowered at him like a wicked moustachioed pantomime uncle and laughed, but he hadn't finished with Michael yet. After the short climb up Anglesea Street he stopped by a garbage can to catch his breath. 'Love, if it were mad enough, could make a man roll around on the floor. Would you agree?'

'I would.' Michael felt himself grow taller in triumph. It was as if he had shouted his love out loud, unafraid and proud as a man should be. Kalazian raised both his fists in the air and shook them. 'That's the spirit,' he said. 'That's the spirit.'

He took Michael by the arm and walked with him bold and confident to the bookshop three doors up from the corner. When they reached it he let go of Michael's arm and faced the door, bowed his head and crossed himself. A dull copper bell attached to a metal coil clacked irritably as he opened the door. Michael wondered if he was expected to cross himself before entering but Kalazian waved him inside. 'Come in,' he said. 'I've frightened away all the evil spirits.'

On the counter immediately to the left of the door was a sign written large in Kalazian's copperplate hand: 'Feel Free to Browse'. Another sign next to it said, 'If you don't see what you want — please enquire.' There was a small brass bell alongside it and next to that a bible-sized book with gold-edged pages and the title *Anthology of Demons*. It was opened at a colour plate of Kali, black, blood-spattered, with fangs and matted hair, corpse earrings and stinking of the slaughterhouse. Michael wanted to close the book to stop Kali from jumping out and biting him and giving him her disease.

'Tea?' Kalazian called from behind a shelf at the back of the shop.

'I thought you'd frightened away all the evil spirits,' said Michael.

With an electric kettle in his hand, Kalazian peered quizzically around the edge of the shelf. Michael pointed at the book and Kalazian laughed. 'Kali's not evil. She's misunderstood.'

Michael gave a quick glance at Kali to make sure she wasn't about to move. 'She looks evil to me.'

Hidden behind the shelf again, Kalazian filled up the kettle and above the rush and howl of the water shouted, 'It's all an illusion, Michael. All an illusion.'

'Try telling that to the victims of Auschwitz,' Michael muttered, as his employer came from behind the shelf wiping his hands on a small handtowel. The smile on his face turned to a frown. 'Michael,' he said, 'if it upsets you that much, turn the page.'

Michael coughed to cover his embarrassment. 'No,' he said, 'I'll leave it open.'

The kettle screamed and steam rose up from behind the bookshelf. Kalazian held his thumb and forefinger together, closed his eyes and gave a beatific smile. 'Tea,' he said, 'will be ready in a jiffy; and what a comforting word a "jiffy" is.'

They had gingernuts with the tea; Kalazian eating four to Michael's one. Halfway through a fifth biscuit Kalazian suddenly leaned back in his chair and raised his eyebrows. 'Customer,' he whispered at the clack of the dull copper bell.

Michael jumped up ready to do something, he wasn't quite sure what, to show Kalazian he intended to earn his two hundred dollars a week. But Kalazian motioned him to sit down. 'Gently, gently,' he said. 'Finish your tea. It doesn't do to startle the customers, although,' he stroked his beard and frowned, 'I know this one; a regular.'

Michael turned around just as the customer rang the small brass bell. He brushed the biscuit crumbs, most of them Kalazian's, off his trousers, straightened his tie and with a polished shop assistant manner approached the customer.

'May I help you sir,' he said and was surprised at how naturally the words came to him. He even had the right tone of smug servility. The customer with neatly combed steel-grey hair and steel-grey moustache to match narrowed his eyes through steel-grey glasses. 'Another one,' he said and sneered.

Michael tried to keep the smile on his face. 'I'm sorry,' he said.

'You're the fourth assistant in as many months,' the customer explained. 'What does Kalazian do with you all — eat you or something?' He gave a contemptuous laugh and showed his glistening yellow teeth. 'I ordered a book,' he said. 'Your predecessor, when I called last week, said it would be in today. The name's Solway.' He pushed his glasses further up the bridge of his nose and sniffed.

'Ah yes,' Michael said as if he already knew about the book. He was doing this shop assistant act so well he had the depressing feeling that he was born for it and was never meant to be a philosopher and seeker of wisdom. He walked smoothly to the back of the shop and Kalazian with a merry twinkle-eyed grin handed him a thin hardback book wrapped tightly in brown paper. There was a white sticker on the front and yet another example of Kalazian's copperplate hand. 'Dr Andrew Solway' it said, '$32'.

Dr Solway was shaking when Michael came back to him; not much, a fine tremor of the fingers, barely noticeable as he snatched the book from Michael's hand. He hid it inside his coat and held his arm close to his side as if he had just received the pay-off in a kidnap case. Michael itched to find out what was under the brown paper wrapping. The hair at the crown of Dr Solway's head came undone and stuck up like a signal of his guilt.

'Put it on my account,' he said and patted his hair down.

'Goodbye, Doctor,' Kalazian called but Dr Solway was already out of the door.

Kalazian looked over Michael's shoulder as he entered the $32 in the doctor's account. 'Oh rose thou art sick,' he said. 'The invisible worm that flies in the night, in the howling storm has found out thy crimson bed of joy.' He put his hand on Michael's shoulder and whispered close to his ear, 'And his dark secret love does thy life destroy.'

Michael closed the account book and looked up. He had a vision of himself in a long, dimly lit tunnel where a moaning wind blew all the time and bits of paper flew past so fast he could never reach out and catch one. He screwed his eyes tight shut and gave his head a shake. 'Is that what the book was?' he asked. Straightening the papers at his desk behind the counter, Kalazian turned to Michael and raised his eyebrows. 'A collection of Blake's poetry?' Michael explained.

'No,' said Kalazian and skewered a piece of paper on the spike on top of his desk.

Michael wondered, considering the vision and all, whether Kalazian had actually spoken the poem or if it was part of the vision but Kalazian reassured him by saying, 'The book is called *The Invisible Worm*.'

'What's it about?'

'I don't know. I've never read it.'

'Well,' said Michael, 'who wrote it?'

'It's anonymous.' It was another of Kalazian's games but Michael persisted. 'Are there any other copies?' he asked.

Kalazian spread his arms. 'The whole shop is full of copies. Feel free to browse,' he added distractedly, flicking through a pile of invoices. 'As the assistant manager you should become familiar with the stock.'

After searching for hours, Michael couldn't find a copy of *The Invisible Worm* though the shop was stacked with books which catered — as Kalazian had promised — for the exclusive and eccentric. At the end of the morning they had covered Michael with a corrosive slime that bubbled away the last traces of optimism from his mind and left an empty stare on his face.

'For a philosopher and psychologist,' said Kalazian over a shared lunch of potato fritters and fishcakes piled up on a grease-blotched sheet of greaseproof paper, 'you show a singular lack of understanding of the human mind.'

'There are things in this shop,' Michael was examining a discoloured patch at the edge of his fishcake, 'that aren't human.'

With a mouthful of half-chewed potato fritter, Kalazian laughed. He put his hand to his mouth, swallowed, and wiped his eyes with the cuff of his pullover. 'Everything in this shop,' he said after taking a deep breath, 'is human.' He picked up another fritter and waved it at Michael. 'That's the trouble with you intellectuals. You deny and reject humanity.'

The piece of fishcake in Michael's mouth tasted even better with the spice of an argument to flavour it. 'I don't deny humanity,' he said. 'I know the things in these books, no matter how debased, are part of humanity.'

'That's very understanding and considerate of you,' said Kalazian. He held an upturned tomato sauce bottle in his hand and shook it but nothing came out. Bits of batter clung to his moustache and beard.

'But,' said Michael, choosing out of politeness the smallest fritter, 'you can't accept murder, sadism, cannibalism, genocide and all the other things contaminating this shop.'

'Why not?' asked Kalazian, hitting the bottom of the bottle with the flat of his hand and splotching out the sauce in a corner of the greaseproof paper. Michael wanted to snatch the bottle from his hand. It wasn't right to be concerned about tomato sauce when more important things were being discussed.

'Do you think such things are right?' he persisted.

Kalazian picked the biggest fritter and dipped it in the sauce. 'Right and wrong have nothing to do with it.' He bit off the end of the fritter before the sauce had time to drip from it. 'If we accept only what we think is right and reject what we think is wrong a whole world of experience is denied us.'

'But we can't all go around murdering and torturing.' Michael wondered if Kalazian would mind if he dipped the end of his fritter in the sauce.

Kalazian shrugged as if Michael's ideas weren't worth answering. 'It's as well for me that not all people think as you, otherwise I'd be out of business.'

'You could always try to cater for the better aspects of humanity.' Michael felt himself blush.

Kalazian wasn't offended. He tapped out some more sauce on the corner of the paper closest to Michael and smiled benevolently. 'I could do that, I suppose. But it's been my experience that people are far more prepared to pay higher prices for their vices than they are for their virtues. Take you, for example.' He handed Michael a cold can of Lemon and Paeroa.

Michael bent his head down to hide another blush and picked at the ring-pull on top of the can.

'You are a virtuous man,' Kalazian went on. 'A seeker of wisdom and truth.'

Michael jerked the ring-pull and it came away with a click and fizz, indicating he wasn't all that virtuous.

'And yet,' said Kalazian, 'you have vices.'

'Who hasn't?' Immediately in some stupid misconception left over from adolescence, he thought of masturbation.

'I'm not talking about wanking,' Kalazian said and Michael's forehead went cold.

Kalazian snatched up the greaseproof paper, bashed it between his hands until it formed a rough ball and tossed it over the back of his head at the wastepaper basket in the corner. It missed. 'I'm talking about another vice,' he said.

Michael thought he heard the shop bell clack and looked up hopefully. There was nobody there. A slow poison was working through his intestines and he was frightened that if he opened his mouth to speak a squeak would come out.

'*The Invisible Worm*,' said Kalazian.

Michael swallowed. His voice didn't come out with a squeak

but it sounded strange, as if it didn't belong to him. 'I told you,' he said. 'I couldn't find a copy.'

'Really?' Kalazian stroked his beard and opened his eyes wide in disbelief. 'For a man with your particular vice I'd have thought the shelves would have been full of copies.'

Michael craned his neck above the counter to see if a rescuing customer was approaching. There was a man outside the shop with his hands deep inside his trouser pockets and a glum expression on his face as he stared at the sign on the door. 'The sign says "Closed",' Kalazian explained as the man trudged off. 'I didn't want any interruptions.'

The eager young shop assistant in Michael insisted, 'We've lost a customer.'

'Don't worry. He'll be back and ten times as keen for having been turned away; that's the way people are with their vices.'

It was about time Michael started to show some well-justified anger. Not too vigorously though; he didn't want his temper to deprive him of two hundred dollars a week. 'Mr Kalazian,' he began slowly and carefully.

'Call me Edward,' Kalazian beamed at him.

'Edward,' said Michael, not so slowly or carefully.

'Don't look so worried. I can see you're angry, so out with it. Say what you like, I'm quite determined to keep you as my assistant manager at two hundred dollars a week.'

'All right,' Michael jumped up with his fists clenched. 'What's all this about invisible worms and secret vices.'

Kalazian nodded thoughtfully then spread his hands. 'Michael,' he said. 'There's no need to be upset. I'm your friend. I only want to become better acquainted with you. Isn't that what friends do?'

He had a confused, hurt look about him which Michael didn't believe. There was an attraction to Kalazian which he found very difficult to resist but he knew part or maybe the whole of that attraction was that Kalazian was dangerous for him. He had the feeling his employer could see him now naked and shivering in some damp corner. 'Friends don't usually make a fuss about each other's vices,' he said cautiously.

Kalazian stood up, stretched his arms above his head and opened his mouth in a luxurious yawn. Half of his lower back teeth on both sides were missing. He smoothed down his pullover and said, 'You're right, of course. You must forgive me, Michael. It's one of my vices, I'm afraid; ferreting about inside other people's heads. How Mrs Kalazian has tolerated me all these years I don't know.'

He sidled past Michael and with his hand poised went straight to the middle aisle, picked out a small red book and gave it to him. 'There you are,' he said. 'Just as I told you: *The Invisible Worm*.'

He sidled past Michael again and turned the 'Closed' sign over. 'I'll leave you to it. The keys are under the counter and the bicycle's around the back.' With a wave and a clack of the door bell he was gone.

4

At five o'clock, not quite on the dot, Michael closed up the bookshop and cycled back to Kingsland. On his way he had to stop once outside Uncle's Hamburger Bar on the Great North Road to pump up the front tyre. A young Maori, wearing a black beret and an ex-Navy greatcoat down to his ankles, eyed him over the top of a half-eaten hamburger. Michael thought he knew him from somewhere and the young Maori nodded as if to confirm this. Thin and stoop-shouldered, with eyes that tried to burn their way out of his head, he could easily have fitted the classic picture of a consumptive but Michael couldn't remember him from the hospital. When he came to think of it, he couldn't recall anyone at the hospital who did actually fit the classic picture of a consumptive. He tested the tyre with his finger. A car drove past with the side window wound down and somebody shouted 'Yah' at him. He looked up but the car was too fast for him to see who it was.

'You know them?' The young Maori was standing directly alongside him now with one last mouthful of hamburger to go.

Michael straightened up the bicycle, shrugged and said, 'No,' as if he hadn't really noticed the car.

'Right now.' The Maori brought his head forward and stared hard at the bridge of Michael's nose. 'Right now, you want to kill them. Right?'

'I don't even know them,' Michael said but the Maori was right. Right now, before fear and conscience had time to dissuade him, he did want to kill whoever was in the car.

'I know them,' said the Maori but Michael didn't believe him. He was up to something. Michael decided he was a bit mad but didn't want to ride off just yet. It would make an intriguing story to tell Anna that night. Anna was a bit mad too. In fact when he thought of it, everyone he'd met recently was a bit mad.

'Give me ten dollars,' the Maori said, 'and I'll fix them for you.'

So that was it. Michael smiled but the Maori didn't stop staring at the bridge of his nose. It was time he left but the Maori wouldn't let him go.

'All right,' he said. 'Forget the ten dollars. I'll do it for five.'

Michael wondered if the front tyre needed pumping up again. 'I don't want anything done.'

'You won't get caught.' The Maori looked quickly behind him. The bald hamburger man was busy scraping grease off the hotplate. 'I'd do it for free, but five dollars isn't much, is it? For something you want done?'

Michael pulled out a five-dollar note from his top pocket and an extra two besides and gave them to the Maori, who grinned. 'Good as done,' he said and backed away.

'The only thing that's as good as done,' said Michael, 'is me,' and rode off even though the front tyre was losing air.

Freewheeling down Bond Street within sight of Kalazian's Boarding House, his face smarting in the wind suddenly went cold. He took one hand from the handlebar, patted the side pocket of his coat and closed his eyes in thanks. The Maori wasn't a pickpocket as well as a con man. What Kalazian had called *The Invisible Worm* was still there. It wasn't really *The Invisible Worm* of course, that was Kalazian's metaphorical title: the invisible worm growing fatter by the day on Michael's secret vice that Kalazian with all his strange powers knew all about and Michael without those strange powers knew nothing about and had to be given little books to frighten him with the truth.

He forced the pedals down as Bond Street rose to meet New North Road. A row of broken-windowed grey concrete tenement houses on the corner had had their backs smashed in since he and Kalazian passed them that morning. Michael didn't know the title of the book in his pocket. He had made a point of not knowing it. When Kalazian gave it to him he had put it straight into his pocket without looking at it and that's where it had stopped all day. Kalazian, barring his way at the bottom of the stairs, would ask what he thought of the book and Michael would say, truthfully, he hadn't got around to reading it yet. He didn't need to read it. He knew what his secret vice was and it wasn't, as Kalazian had already said, wanking. He laughed to himself as he stopped at the traffic lights and a little boy in the car alongside him with his runny nose against the window stared at him with bush-baby eyes.

Outside the Kingsland Motorcycle Shop the bike maniacs all unshaven in leather jackets and Wehrmacht boots stopped their talk of rape and drugs and loud noises and sneered at Michael as he rode past. A low-browed Morris 1100 heading vacant-eyed towards the city nearly clipped his rear wheel as he turned into Central Avenue. If he'd been run over and killed the driver would probably never know that he had also squashed an invisible worm. Michael laughed again. His secret vice was nothing to be given secret books about. It was simple enough, and not all that secret. Kalazian found it impossible to avoid indulging in supercilious and cryptic games but if he had been more straightforward and honest, Michael, after some thought, could have told him.

'My secret vice, Mr Kalazian,' he would have said in the same triumphant tone he had used to announce his love for Anna, 'is the great vice of the modern world — voyeurism.'

With the front tyre almost flat he dismounted the bicycle while it was still in motion and ran with it to the door of the Kalazian's Boarding House where he stopped out of breath but victorious. Kalazian would be waiting at the bottom of the stairs stroking the knob on the banister in that suggestive way of his. Well, he could slink back to his kitchen and cook up another dish; the poison in this one hadn't worked. He wheeled the bicycle around the back of the house and opened the door to the laundry.

Mr Charles was there, sitting on a small stool watching the rags and tatters of his life tumble around in the drier. Busy with his fantasy, Michael pretended not to notice him but Mr Charles jumped up and nearly knocked the stool over. 'Oh,' he said with one hand on his chest and trying to force a smile which wouldn't stay on his face, 'you startled me.'

He had a thin piece of sticking plaster across the tip of his nose. 'I'm sorry,' said Michael. He parked the bicycle tidily as Kalazian had instructed, behind the laundry door, and tried to think what came next in the drama of Kalazian's defeat but Mr Charles was persistent.

'Oh no really,' he said. 'It's I who should be sorry. I mean . . .' He giggled and smoothed the already smooth lapels on his velvet shirt. 'I seem to make a fool of myself whenever we meet, although . . .' He giggled again. 'We haven't really met, have we? I mean, formally.'

His fantasy disappearing like a dot on a switched-off television, Michael was in no mood for formal introductions. Mr Charles mumbled, 'Gordon Charles,' but kept his hand behind his back. Michael was sure he could hear Kalazian pacing about on the floor above.

'Michael O'Sullivan,' he held out his hand quickly without thinking. Mr Charles took it eagerly.

'Very pleased to meet you,' he said as the drier switched off behind him with a snap and a mutter. He half turned towards it but wouldn't let go of Michael's hand.

'I think your clothes are ready,' Michael managed to pull his hand free. Mr Charles darted across to the drier.

'You're very kind,' he said, gripping the drier at the side and peering into its window. 'I can see that. Not many people shake my hand these days although . . .' He patted the drier. 'I'm not diseased or anything. I've had myself checked out, so it's all right. There's no need to worry.'

Michael thought he heard Kalazian thumping along the corridor back to his kitchen.

'Anyway.' Mr Charles didn't seem able to stop chattering as he pulled his clothes from the drier. 'You can't get it from handshakes.' His eyes glittered as he stretched his underpants between his splayed-out fingers.

Michael tried to slip out quietly without opening the laundry door too wide but Mr Charles let out a gasp and stopped him.

'Oh no,' he said as if he'd just remembered the iron full on upstairs and scorching its way through his silk pyjamas. His fingers tapped frantically at his lower lip. 'I've done it again. I'm sorry. Please, you've got to forgive me. You've no idea how sorry I am. You will forgive me, won't you?' He dropped his arms disconsolately to his sides and hung his head. Michael didn't wonder that someone had been provoked into hitting Mr Charles but said yes all the same.

Mr Charles brought his head up with a grin, said a cheery thank you and, humming to himself, started to fold his clothes neatly. Michael opened the door wide, walked out and slammed it behind him. He'd be lucky to catch Kalazian now.

As he walked around the side of the house the sun, struggling to stay afloat, swelled and turned red then with no one to help, sank behind the Waitakeres for the two hundred and thirty-first time that year. By the time he had worked that out he was at the bottom of the stairs. Kalazian, tired of waiting, was in his kitchen cooking up a vindaloo and singing the toreador's song from *Carmen*, or at least his garbled version of it, at the top of his voice. Michael could see Mrs Kalazian sitting at the kitchen table with her hands over her ears and a magazine in front of her, its open pages pinned down by her elbows.

At the top of the stairs the kukri was missing from its scabbard and Mallis was leaving Anna's room, his back to Michael and his shirt-tail showing below his pullover. Michael felt very light. All the water in his body evaporated leaving a powder that disappeared like sand through a funnel in the floor. He would have ceased to exist if it hadn't been for the weight of the book in his pocket, holding him down. Anna stood in her doorway in a dressing gown with her hair undone and her face turned towards Mallis. Michael stepped back against the wall at the top of the stairs but she heard him; his heart clawed about inside him like something in a cage.

'Michael?' she brushed back a lock of hair from her forehead. Mallis at the other end of the corridor went into his room and didn't turn around once.

'I didn't hear you,' Anna said.

There wasn't a trace of shame about her. She was wearing nothing under her long blue dressing gown and nothing on her feet but a pair of slip-on slippers. Not ten minutes before, while Michael was trying to keep his script alive under Mr Charles's attack, Anna had been naked with Mallis; stretched out on her bed with a dreamy look on her face and Mallis gloating over her body with his greasy black hair and doing things to her with the stolen kukri. Michael tried a laugh, but it fell on the floor like a broken plate. He kicked it to one side.

'I didn't want to embarrass you,' he said and managed to walk to his door without tripping up.

'Embarrass?' Anna wrinkled her brow as if he was speaking Bulgarian, then suddenly laughed.

He was expecting some explanation from her; some perfectly simple, mundane explanation as to what a man with greasy black hair and his shirt-tail hanging out and a stolen kukri was doing in her room, with her naked under her dressing gown and only a pair of slip-on slippers on her feet.

'Our date's still on for tonight, is it?' said Anna.

'Yes. I thought I'd ring out for a pizza if that's all right.'

'Sounds great,' said Anna. 'I've a bottle of red wine somewhere.'

'Good.' Michael put his key in the keyhole the wrong way up.

'See you then,' said Anna and closed her door quietly so that the lock didn't click. That was thoughtful of her. A click on top of everything else would have been more than Michael could bear.

Back in his room waiting for the pizza to arrive and unable to re-inflate the optimism that had kept him afloat since leaving hospital, Michael succumbed to temptation. His coat, hanging on a peg from the back of the door, began to annoy him. It hung down too much on one side. He took Kalazian's book out and threw it on the bed, then tugged at the coat until it hung straight and the folds on each side matched. Fortunately the book had landed face down; there was nothing on its red cover to betray what it was. When he picked it up, intent on putting it out of harm's way, still face down, in the drawer of his bedside locker, he stopped as he felt its weight in his hand. It was very curious. He hadn't noticed it before but now, in the quiet of his room and the concentration of his mind on things not quite right, the book felt strange; too light for its size. Carefully avoiding any accidental glance at the spine or the front and keeping the front and back firmly pinched together to stop the pages falling open, he glanced at the top of the book. The pages were too white and he knew without opening it why the book was too light. Kalazian had played a trick on him. It wasn't a book at all. There was nothing in it; the pages were blank.

With the truth out there was no harm in having a look at the front of the book. In spite of his melancholy mood he laughed to himself when he saw there was nothing written on the front or the spine either. Every page was blank; not even a number at the top. He suddenly felt like running downstairs and shaking Kalazian's hand and having a good laugh with him. It was a great joke and an even better one for showing Kalazian had gone to the trouble of observing him and understanding him and trusting him enough to know he wouldn't mind having a joke played on him. He went over to the mirror and poked his tongue out at himself. Invisible worms and dark hidden secrets, unmentionable vices; he almost laughed out loud. Evil lying in wait with its long dirty fingernails under the crimson bed of joy, for crying out loud. He looked closer at himself in the mirror. Out of the tip of his nose grew a tiny black hair. He went cross-eyed trying to pull it out between his finger and thumb but the hair stayed where it was; a symbol of Kalazian's wisdom. A red book or a tiny black hair on the end of your nose serve their purpose as well as a blinding conversion on the road to Damascus.

Kalazian was very wise and very cunning. If it hadn't been for Mr Charles delaying him, Michael, in his enthusiasm to outwit Kalazian, would have betrayed himself, confessed his secret vice, argued that it was no vice, declared his innocence, protested at the accusation all the while swelling up like bubblegum, with Kalazian's smile growing wider and wider until the bubble burst. He would naturally apologise to Kalazian for depriving him of that pleasure.

He was so pleased with himself he tore the sticking plaster off his hand sure that the cut from the kukri had healed. It hadn't. Pale pink fluid trickled from it, down his wrist. He stuck the plaster back on and pretended he hadn't taken it off but it didn't stick very well. He wondered if Anna would put a new one on for him and tell him what was going on between her and Mallis; not that it was any of his business. He didn't own her. Tomorrow, when he gave the book back to Kalazian and they had laughed together as friends do when they have played jokes on each other, he might ask Kalazian's opinion on love.

Mrs Kalazian knocked at his door and told him the pizza man had arrived. Walking down the stairs with Michael she said she didn't much like being disturbed from her meal to run messages for tenants. Her breath when she spoke was scented with coriander and chillies, garlic and ghee, garam masala, vinegar and cinnamon from Varanasi where everyone slept on the rooftops at night and thieves went about their business in the alleyways.

'I'm sorry,' Michael said. 'It won't happen again.'

'Edward calls you a thinker,' Mrs Kalazian said as she stepped off the bottom step, 'but as far as I can see you're as thoughtless as anyone else your age.'

The pizza was very good; *capricciosa* with spicy salami and olives, pastry just the right thickness and crispy on the outside. It made no difference though; Michael still longed for a taste of Kalazian's vindaloo and Anna didn't tell him what she and Mallis were doing together. Even after three glasses of Valpolicella she still didn't mention it. Suggesting that he shouldn't have picked at his cut, she was content to sit back on three cushions and listen to her music; Pink Floyd this time and not quite as scratched as Joe Cocker. The faint lines at the corners of her eyes as she sat beside him were there when she was born, already knowing everything, into an old and familiar world.

The record finished and the turntable switched off with a click. Over by the fireplace the gas fire hissed, impatient for someone to break the silence. 'You could always ask me,' Anna said without turning her head.

A 'what?' escaped from Michael's mouth before he had time to stop it. Anna undid the drawstring on the neck of her chemise and Michael wondered if he was supposed to make some sort of sexual advance.

'Whatever's on your mind,' said Anna, and tied the drawstring in a neater bow.

She knew what was on his mind. There was no need to ask him. 'I've no right to ask,' he said.

Still without turning her head, Anna asked, 'Do you love me?' It was no timid request for reassurance but a direct, straightfoward question.

'Yes,' said Michael.

'Then,' said Anna, 'you've a right.'

With permission to ask, Michael had no idea what to say. He didn't want to reveal himself as jealous, suspicious, immature, unsophisticated, insecure; all the things he knew himself to be and all the things a woman like Anna would wish he wasn't. If only he had the time to dart downstairs to ask Kalazian's advice. A man of the world like Kalazian would know what to do.

'What was Mallis doing in my room?' Anna saved him the trouble. 'Is he my lover? Did we have sex?' At last she looked at Michael.

He looked away and nodded.

She put her hand on top of his and he showed he wasn't absolutely immature by not snatching his own hand away.

'Eddie tells me you're a seeker of knowledge.'

In spite of his efforts, Michael could feel a pout coming on. Remembering what Mrs Kalazian had told him, he mumbled, 'Eddie seems to have told everyone what I am.'

'I haven't had sex with Mallis for a long time,' said Anna. 'He was never my lover and I was never his.'

Michael shook his head. He believed Anna, but that wasn't the point. He had been dishonest; smiling when Anna opened the door to him, asking what sort of a day she had had and not listening to her answer, gossiping about Mr Charles and what an irritating person he was and all the while wanting to ask her the questions she had just asked and answered herself.

'I'm sorry,' he said.

'What for?' Anna laughed. 'You haven't manipulated me into telling you anything I didn't want to tell you. I'd have told you earlier but you were too busy sulking and glaring at me.'

'Was I?'

'And now that you do know,' said Anna, 'are you glad?'

'No,' said Michael. 'It was none of my business.'

'I've told you already.' Anna stood up. Bits of pizza pastry crust fell from her skirt. Michael had an urge to pick them up and eat them.

'It's your business,' Anna took the record off the turntable, holding it on the edge with the fingertips of both hands. 'You can love me if you like,' she said as she flipped the record over. 'It won't make any difference; I'll still be dead.'

She was mad. Along with the lines on her face and the warmth of her smell, she was mad. Michael brushed the pizza crumbs under her cushion.

'You're not dead,' he said.
'Not yet,' said Anna, 'but soon.'
She sat down beside Michael in time for the start of side two.

5

It's all very well having recovered from an illness that a hundred years ago killed most people who caught it, and it's all very well having a job in a bookshop and the grain in your oak furniture full of rivers and eyes and naked women, and it's all very well being a seeker of wisdom and knowledge with a friend like Kalazian to guide you and encourage you, but in the small hours of the morning, when the woman you love has seen you to the door after letting you make love to her and been so full of life and feeling you can't believe she's mad and says mad things, it's easy to see that the lives of three or four little people don't amount to a hill of beans in this crazy world.

First thing tomorrow, Michael decided and switched off his bedside lamp, he'd have it out with Mallis. The man was obviously some sort of evil mastermind, cruelly twisting Anna's already distorted ideas to suit his own purposes. He was a sadist or a masochist or most likely a sado-masochist. People like him ought to be locked up. With his mind made up and his resolve firm as a hero's handshake, self-righteously he fell asleep and in next to no time awoke with his resolve in tatters. Mallis had appeared to him in a dream and tapped him on the shoulder with the tip of the kukri. Michael was sure he had never had sex with him and never been his lover. Mallis was his friend and companion on a journey to somewhere important. Mallis meant him no harm and offered, in the friendliest way imaginable, to slice Michael's head off.

Sweating, he sat up in bed. For a second or two he thought he was back in the hospital and listened for the sounds of coughing and snoring and farting and a nurse padding around in gym shoes with a torch in her hand. He thumped his chest twice and coughed and took some time to convince himself he was well. Mallis, he now knew, would not be so easy to deal with. A man capable of sneaking into your dreams at night was not to be dismissed so lightly. Michael heard a toilet flush downstairs and muffled voices coming up through the floorboards. He turned over in bed, pulled the blankets around his shoulders and tried to sleep but the staircase creaked. He sat up. Someone was breathing outside his door; standing there, listening. If Michael was to creep quietly across to the door and open it there wouldn't be anyone there. There never was in these sort of movies. He would look up and down the corridor and there wouldn't be anyone there either. The scene would tell people watching the movie that his nerves were on edge and his imagination playing tricks. He crept quietly to the door and opened it. Mallis was there breathing through his hairy nostrils. Michael screwed his eyes tight shut but when he opened them Mallis was still there. He had one hand behind his back and a grin on his face. Michael could hear the Kalazians whispering to each other at the bottom of the stairs. Mallis watched his eyes closely and seemed about to pounce.

'What . . . ?' said Michael but got no further. Mallis brought his hand from behind his back and held the kukri at his side with the blade pointing down. Michael jumped back, slammed the door and locked it. He went straight back to bed and straight back to sleep and dreamed that he wrote something in Kalazian's book. When he awoke he checked the book and sure enough there was writing in it; two pages of badly scrawled blue ballpoint. Before he had time to read the first word he awoke and checked the book and sure enough it was blank.

The book was still blank when he handed it to Kalazian, busy eating porridge at the kitchen table. Kalazian sprinkled more sugar on his porridge and without looking up from his bowl handed the book back to Michael.

'There's nothing in it,' said Michael.

'Really?' said Kalazian and pushed the empty bowl to one side. 'I would have thought you'd have written something in it by now. Something of a confessional nature. *The Secret Life of M* might be a good working title.'

'I haven't got a secret life. At least nothing that requires confession.'

Kalazian poured himself a cup of tea. He raised his eyebrows and the pot at Michael.

'No thanks.'

Kalazian took a slurp from the cup and smacked his lips. 'Stewed to perfection,' he said.

'Besides,' said Michael, 'I don't want to get tangled up in another one of your rope tricks. I just wanted to give the book back and ask if you've got a puncture repair kit anywhere.'

'I'll tell you what.' Kalazian emptied the slops from his saucer into his cup. 'It's easy to see you're not used to this sort of thing. I'll get you started.'

He was paying two hundred dollars a week with a bicycle thrown in and this reminded Michael. 'I could buy a repair kit myself,' he said, 'if you haven't got one.'

Kalazian looked up at the ceiling for inspiration, found it and snapped his fingers. 'How does this sound?' He spoke as if he was dictating to an amanuensis (whatever that is). 'Last night,' he went on, 'I made love to the woman I love; Anna in brackets. She asked me afterwards if I would kill her. I think I will.'

Michael laughed. 'I don't like brackets.'

Kalazian swallowed his tea in a single gulp and looked in the bottom of his cup. 'All right,' he said, 'but without the brackets, what do you think. Accurate enough, wouldn't you say?'

'Apart from the lovemaking,' Michael looked at his watch, 'not at all accurate. There was no mention of killing.'

'But,' said Kalazian and pointed to the drawer at the end of the draining board, 'she mentioned death, didn't she . . . specifically her own?'

'Yes.' At Kalazian's insistent pointing, he went over to the drawer.

'Well,' said Kalazian, 'there you are; same thing. She wants you to kill her.'

Michael opened the drawer. A small flat tin was inside with 'Puncture Repair Kit' written on it. He took the lid off. There was rubber solution, patches and French chalk. 'An old kit,' he remarked, 'but then it's an old bicycle.'

'It is indeed,' said Kalazian. 'Almost as ancient as man's desire to possess the thing he loves and so to destroy it.' There was no shaking him off.

'Anna,' Michael said as he put the puncture repair kit in his pocket, 'doesn't want me to kill her.'

'Oh but she does. She longs for it. You can see it in her eyes. Don't tell me you can't see it, Michael.'

Michael didn't answer. His mouth went dry and the muscles at the back of his neck tightened. He could feel his head start to shake. He looked away from Kalazian who was using the trick of staring at the bridge of the nose again.

'Michael,' said Kalazian with a voice as soft as a priest's from behind a confessional grille. 'Do you love Anna?'

'I've a puncture to repair,' said Michael, but his voice quavered at the edges.

'Do you love her?' Kalazian insisted.

Michael looked up and said, 'Yes.'

'Then,' said Kalazian and sighed, 'why won't you give her what she wants?'

'Because I love her.' Even to Michael it sounded too lame. It didn't mean anything.

'You wouldn't get caught. I've got it all worked out.'

Michael relaxed his shoulders and took a deep breath. It stopped his head shaking long enough for him to say, 'This is another of your tricks, Kalazian, like all that rubbish about invisible worms and secret vices.'

'Please.' Kalazian frowned that Michael could think so ill of him. 'Call me Edward.'

'All right,' said Michael. 'This is another one of your tricks, Edward.'

'Perhaps it is. My life is so full of tricks and lies I lose track of them sometimes but it's true what I say, trick or not. You could give Anna what she wants and never be caught. I'd do it myself but,' he raised his eyebrows and shrugged, 'I don't love her the way you do; not enough, that is, to kill her.'

'You're mad.'

'As mad as anyone who has no delusions.'

Michael's throat was so dry his voice came out like a broken tea pot. 'I don't want to kill her.'

'But you do,' said Kalazian. 'You long for it. I can see it in your eyes.'

Michael wished with all his might, or what little might he had left, that he was an ordinary man to whom ordinary things happened, like a puncture in the front tyre of his bicycle, for instance. He wanted to be worried about getting to work on time and discovered to his relief that he was worried about getting to work on time.

'I'll be late,' he said.

'I'm sure the boss won't mind,' said Kalazian and Michael was crestfallen.

'Michael,' said Kalazian as kind as a cup of cocoa, 'I can see I've upset you with all this talk.' He waved his hand as if the talk was nothing.

'I'm not a murderer.'

Kalazian tutted. 'Absolutely not,' he said. 'A murderer has malice aforethought and there is no malice in you.'

Michael felt tired. The game was over for the time being. 'You're very kind,' he said.

'I'm not, you know.'

'But you know I could never kill,' said Michael.

'I didn't say that,' said Kalazian and he hadn't either.

Mallis of course had malice aforethought and he demonstrated it well when he came during the lunch break to Kalazian's bookshop. Michael was sitting on the wooden steps at the back of the shop. Rangitoto Island on the near horizon, looking like the tip of a tricorn hat, tried to nudge its way through the city buildings in order to make his acquaintance.

Mallis frightened it off when he pushed open the door in the fence at the back of the shop yard. Michael screwed up the chip wrapping paper on his lap and jumped to his feet. Mallis had a stick in his hand. It looked like a walking stick, polished ebony with a smooth bone handle, but was obviously a sword-stick. Michael was prepared to leap off the steps and make his escape over the back fence before Mallis had time to unsheath the sword and run him through.

'Sorry to interrupt your lunch break,' said Mallis from the bottom step.

'That's all right,' Michael mumbled and wondered if the jump from the steps might twist his ankle.

On the middle step, Mallis continued, 'I've come to return this,' and handed the stick, handle first, to Michael.

Perhaps he wanted him to unsheath the sword so that he could run Mallis through? Mallis was after all a sadist or a masochist or most likely a sado-masochist. Michael looked for a catch or a clip at the base of the handle but couldn't see one.

'Thanks,' he said, and took the stick.

On the top step Mallis said, 'It belongs in an umbrella stand by the front door.' He was wearing a blue pinstripe jacket frayed at the cuffs and hadn't shaved for at least two days. There was grey among the stubble, though his hair was black and shiny.

'I'll see it's returned to its rightful place.' said Michael. Mallis had him so rattled that he even ended the silly cliché with a strangled giggle. He gave a surreptitious tug of the handle but the stick stayed a stick and he wasn't surreptitious enough.

'There's no need to pretend,' Mallis said.

Michael giggled again. If he wasn't careful he'd soon be gnawing at his knuckles.

'Pretend?' he said in a squeaky voice.

'How's your hand,' asked Mallis, as solicitous as a Gestapo interrogator.

'Hand?' Michael tugged at the stick again. With any luck the blade would come out this time and frighten Mallis away but the stick stayed as it was.

'That was a nasty cut the other night,' said Mallis. 'Very nasty.' He almost licked his lips at how nasty it was.

'It was an accident.'

Mallis closed his eyes and nodded. 'The stick,' he said, 'is a stick; nothing there to cut yourself on.'

Michael took a deep breath to compose himself but it didn't work. He glanced quickly at his watch. 'It's time I opened the shop.'

'Kalazian,' said Mallis and stopped Michael dead. 'Kalazian gave me that stick as a mark of his friendship.' He snorted at the idea. 'He thinks he knows me. Kalazian thinks he knows everybody. He thinks he knows you.'

When Mallis said this he turned and stepped down to the middle step. 'He wants you to kill Anna.' He looked over his shoulder at Michael and laughed. 'Don't worry, you're not the first one he's tried to seduce. Including me you're the fourth one I know.' He stepped on to the bottom step and without turning said almost to himself, 'He might have miscalculated this time.'

Michael gripped the stick tight in his hand. He was going mad. He could feel it. The back of Mallis's head would split like a watermelon if he hit it hard enough. Mallis turned to face him just in time.

'You,' he said, 'might be the one to do it.'

Mallis was in on the trick with Kalazian; that much was certain. 'Absolute bloody rubbish,' Michael shouted and Mallis shrugged.

Below the steps, growing up through the cracks in the paving, were dock and nettles and dandelions with shrivelled heads. They stank of cat's piss and all the despair of ruined places. Things, Michael admitted, were finally going very wrong. It was almost a comfort to be back in the familiar world of lies and deceit and poisoned air. The bookshop had no hidden secrets or invisible worms. It was full of trash and pornography like any other trashy, pornographic, sleazy little bookshop. Anna was not strange or romantically doomed. She, he now knew, was in on Kalazian's trick too. She wasn't going to die and he wasn't going to kill her. And Kalazian himself, manipulative and clever, playing some joke to alleviate the boredom and guilt of living out of his wife's purse. Well it was a good joke; very funny, ha, ha, ha. He certainly had Michael fooled. And now to top it off here was Mallis in on the act to tell him all portentous and dramatic, 'You might be the one to do it.' Ha, ha, ha. To top even that, Mallis was right.

Mallis was over at the gate now and halfway through it. Michael laughed out loud; three times, one after the other, aimed like bricks at the back of Mallis's head. Mallis shrugged again and was out of the gate down the back alley and away.

When Kalazian visited the bookshop that afternoon he was red in the face and breathing hard. His usual composure had deserted him and Michael was glad. He was going to have it out with Kalazian: confront him and accuse him of being a sadist or a masochist or most likely a sado-masochist. He was glad to see Kalazian the way he was; red-faced and deserted he wouldn't be as full of tricks. He was even more pleased when Kalazian glanced at the umbrella stand and groaned. Michael rose to his full height; the confrontation about to begin.

Kalazian grabbed his arm and he could feel his hand shaking. 'Michael,' he said. 'How's business?'

'Brisk.' He pulled his arm from Kalazian's grasp. 'Very brisk. I never realised there was such a demand for poison.'

'Oh Michael.' For all his beard and bulk Kalazian was almost abject. 'I know you're angry with me and you've every right to be. I play tricks, I talk too much. I don't mean to.' He examined his beautifully manicured nails. 'It's a character flaw, I suppose.'

Michael sighed loudly.

'But I don't do anything,' Kalazian insisted. 'That's the trouble. I talk of all the wriggly things that seethe inside our minds. I've got a whole shop full of wriggly things, but it's all talk, all words. I don't do anything. I can't. I surround myself with images but reality terrifies me.'

Michael clenched his fists, closed his eyes and gritted his teeth. Beneath his apologies Kalazian was up to his tricks again. He heard the dull clack of the doorbell. When he opened his eyes Kalazian was already outside holding the door open for him.

'Close up the shop, Michael,' he said.

Michael stayed where he was.

'It's the wriggly things, Michael.' Kalazian stood there. 'One of them's escaped.'

6

On the footpath at the side of the house, beneath Anna's window, was an eye. It looked like a hard-boiled egg with bits of raggedy mincemeat stuck on the sides. Mr Charles, in a pair of light blue corduroy trousers, kept guard from a safe distance, sitting on a canvas chair with a stick in his hand.

'To keep the dogs off,' he explained. 'I daren't touch it. I know I'd just die if I did.'

Anna's window was open. Down in the gully where the motorway ran, trucks and motorbikes and cars snarled and whined after each other. Michael stepped carefully around the safety zone set up by Mr Charles, to the front of the eye. Half the iris showed above the gravel path. It looked sad and surprised. There was a dull silver film over it but it was hazel all right. The footpath and the eye blurred and melted and when Michael put his hand to his face his cheeks were wet.

'I was on my way to the laundry,' Mr Charles said, 'when it landed, plop, right in front of me. I nearly trod on it.' He had to raise his voice to catch Michael who ran down the path towards the front door. 'There are some sick people in this world, I can tell you.'

If he had any sense, Michael thought as he took the stairs two at a time, he'd go straight to his room and straight out with his pack packed, then off up the road and on to the first bus with a number where the digits didn't add up to nine or six. By the next morning he would be well away in Palmerston North or New Plymouth, somewhere where everybody lived in nice little houses and nobody, not even in their wildest nightmares, would ever scoop out one of their eyes and throw it out of the window.

'She's in there,' said Mrs Kalazian outside Anna's door. Her arms were folded and there was a grim look on her face. 'I can hear her bumping into the furniture.'

'Have you got a master key?' Michael didn't care if Mrs Kalazian saw him with tears in his eyes.

'It's locked with the key in the lock,' said Mrs Kalazian. 'She won't open it and the men here are useless.' On the floor by her slipper-shod feet was an enamel basin chipped around the rim; it was filled with hot water and a sponge and a roll of bandage lay beside it.

Michael knelt down and called Anna's name through the keyhole. 'Open the door, please,' he said. He could hear her shuffling about inside as if she was feeling her way around the walls.

'Michael,' Mrs Kalazian said. 'Stop buggering about.'

With four kicks the door burst off its lock. Mrs Kalazian was in first with the water and bandages. Anna was over at the far wall by the window. She stroked it and patted it and listened as if she was searching for a secret passage. Michael wiped his eyes with the heel of his hand. He wanted to take Anna away and tell her lies that would make her well but behind his compassion he wondered what an empty eye socket looked like.

'Shouldn't we call an ambulance or something?' he said with his arms hanging uselessly at his sides.

Mrs Kalazian, with the enamel bowl on the sideboard and unwrapping the bandage, said, 'There's no need for ambulances. This is a respectable house.'

There wasn't much blood, considering; a splotch on the floor and a smear on the windowpane. It was Anna's right eye on the footpath outside. The eyelids had been sucked into the empty socket and came together in the middle, the eyelashes intertwining and sealed with yellow grease. It was very efficient. Mrs Kalazian wouldn't have much cleaning up to do; a small amount of watery stuff leaking out at the edge and a bit of dried blood on the cheek, that was all. There was the other eye of course. That was still where it was supposed to be but the lids had closed over and were swollen and red.

'Stop staring,' Mrs Kalazian ordered, 'and get her over here on to the bed. And close that window. It's draughty in here.'

When Michael closed the window Mr Charles looked up from shooing off a tentatively sniffing black cat and gave him a wave.

With her dressing gown fallen open at the top and her left shoulder bare, Anna let him guide her over to the bed and said nothing. She smelled so frightened Michael want to lie down with her and, one eye missing or not, have sex with her like he had done over two hundred years ago before the wriggly thing escaped. He had the beginnings of an erection and hoped Mrs Kalazian hadn't noticed. Mrs Kalazian bent over Anna and pushed Michael away gently with her arm.

'Get that thing off the footpath,' she said, 'and burn it.'

Kalazian was at the bottom of the stairs with three sheets of paper towel in his hand.

'I'm cursed,' he announced, 'with the vision of what needs to be done and the inability to do it.' He added in a hurried whisper as Michael snatched the towels off him, 'We must talk.'

'We'll talk,' said Michael, but in the meantime there was something on the footpath that needed to be got rid of. He couldn't understand why Mr Charles was guarding it so jealously or why he looked as if he was about to be sick when Michael picked it up. It was after all only a hard-boiled egg or a half-set jelly. It was such a small thing to do to please his landlady. 'Burn it,' she'd said, so he borrowed a box of matches from Kalazian and started a fire in the incinerator at the back of the back garden. In less than ten seconds, in the middle of the flames, the hard-boiled egg or half-set jelly or whatever it was had fizzed and popped and disappeared. The smoke from the fire made his eyes so red and sore and watery that he could hardly see. Kalazian, his kindly self again, gave Michael four orange capsules shaped like little rugby balls and a glass of water to swallow them with. He felt better almost immediately.

'Don't worry about Anna,' said Kalazian. 'Mrs Kalazian has training and experience in this sort of thing.'

Michael had every confidence in Mrs Kalazian's abilities. 'I'm not worried,' he said. His mind was as clear as a Windolened window.

'We'll postpone our talk for the time being.' Kalazian put the blankets around Michael's shoulders. 'Go to sleep now.' He turned off the lamp and tiptoed to the bedroom door. 'I'll see you in the morning,' he said. 'In the meantime don't worry about a thing.'

'I'm not worried,' murmured Michael and he wasn't either. His mind was so clear he could see right through it. All the clutter and jumble and bits of rubbish had gone; all the rotten apple cores and torn-up newspapers and chewed-up chewing gum and spat-out caramel lollies lying in ambush on the pavement; all gone and all the wriggly things too, all gone. There was nothing to worry about and the sound of the motorway soughing in the distant lulled him off to sleep.

He wasn't worried when he woke and he wasn't worried when he went downstairs in his dressing gown to meet the policemen who had so kindly called to ask him a few routine questions. They spoke in Kalazian's kitchen, 'where I'm sure,' said Kalazian, 'you'll be more comfortable.'

'There's nothing to worry about,' the policemen assured him. 'A few routine questions. It's all routine,' they said and sighed, or at least one of them did. The other stayed in the background with a notebook in his hand and took notes. The surprising thing was they never once mentioned hardboiled eggs or jellies or the possibility that anyone even in their wildest dreams could ever scoop out one of their eyes and throw it out of the window. The one without the notebook, a sergeant, showed him a photograph of a smiling friendly-faced young Maori.

'Do you know this man?' he asked.

With a mug of tea in his hand from the smiling friendly-faced Kalazian, Michael took the photograph, pushed out his bottom lip, shook his head and said, 'No.'

'Are you sure?' insisted the sergeant. He had grey eyes and a finely clipped grey moustache but his fingernails were chewed down to the quick. 'Take a closer look.'

Michael took a closer look and the lid flew off a dustbin in an alley at the back of his otherwise perfectly clear mind. It rattled and clattered and banged up against a lamp-post. The bin fell over and rotten apple cores, bits of newspaper, chewing gum and melted caramel lollies fell out.

Kalazian offered the sergeant and his companion tea but they mumbled a polite refusal, or at least the sergeant did. His companion scribbled in his notebook as if he had never been asked. Michael handed the photograph back to the sergeant.

'No,' he said. 'I don't know this man.'

'And you've never seen him?' The sergeant narrowed his eyes in what Michael supposed was practised scepticism to trap the naïve and unwary.

'I might have seen him,' he said and Kalazian tutted his disapproval. 'All I said,' said Michael, 'was that I didn't know him.'

'So you did,' said the sergeant and his companion made a note of it. Michael caught a glimpse of Mrs Kalazian through the open kitchen door, going up the stairs with a tray in her hand. There was a mug and a breakfast bowl on it and steam rising from both. In front of the bowl was an eggcup with a brown egg in it and Michael wondered if that was tactful.

'So you've seen him?' the sergeant said hot on the trail.

'I said I might have.'

'So you did,' said the sergeant and his companion made a note of it again.

'Two evenings ago,' volunteered Michael. 'Outside Uncle's hamburger place on Great North Road. I had a puncture.'

'Yes,' said the sergeant as if he already knew.

Kalazian sat at the kitchen table with his head down and groaned. The sergeant frowned at him.

'I gave him some money,' Michael said.

'Why?' asked the sergeant as quick as a viper.

'To get rid of him.'

'How much?' the sergeant asked as his companion scribbled to keep up with him.

'I don't know,' Michael shrugged. 'A couple of dollars.'

'There's a witness,' said the sergeant, 'who says he thought it was ten dollars or maybe more.'

The bald hamburger man, thought Michael and resolved never to buy a hamburger from Uncle's on Great North Road.

'It was seven,' he said. 'No more.'

'Did he menace you in any way?' the sergeant asked as if he was politely enquiring after Michael's health. Demanding money with menaces; so that was it. They were trying to build up a case against the friendly-faced Maori, probably at the instigation of the spiteful, malicious and bald hamburger man. Hadn't they better things to do with their time? Didn't they know there was real evil in the world? Michael wondered if Kalazian had any little orange rugby balls left.

'No,' he said. 'He didn't menace me. In fact he was very friendly.' He tried to remember whether he was or not.

'So friendly,' the sergeant said and almost had both hands up ready to pounce, 'that he offered to do you a favour?'

'Sergeant.' Kalazian came to Michael's rescue. 'Are these questions routine? They seem,' he said, scratching his head, 'to have taken on an accusatory tone.'

With a new actor in the script the sergeant's companion looked up from his notebook, nonplussed and perplexed.

'Don't look so nonplussed and perplexed,' Kalazian said. 'The name's Kalazian.' He spelt it out and the sergeant's companion wrote it down.

'If,' the sergeant said between his teeth, 'Mr O'Sullivan could answer for himself.'

Michael was about to answer for himself but Kalazian raised his hand to stop him. 'I can see, sergeant,' he said, 'that you are an experienced and clever man.'

There was a hint of a blush on the sergeant's face but his bristly moustache, obviously grown for the purpose, bristled even more. Kalazian rose from his seat and his pullover seemed to swell to accommodate his bulk.

'I can also see,' he went on, 'that you are full of traps for the naïve and unwary. There should be two dots over the i in naïve,' he added for the benefit of the sergeant's companion.

'Michael, alas, is naïve and unwary. He is liable, in his innocence, to answer questions in such a way that the more cynical among us,' and Kalazian smiled at the sergeant, 'are likely to consider him guilty.'

'If he's innocent,' said the sergeant, 'he has nothing to fear.'

Kalazian laughed. 'Do you really believe that, sergeant?'

'Sir,' the sergeant tried to puff himself up to increase his authority but was no match for Kalazian, 'I am conducting this enquiry. If you would kindly be seated and silent, or better still leave us in private.'

'Michael is my friend.' Kalazian's eyebrows nearly jumped off his forehead. 'I feel I should point out to you, sergeant, that I have had legal training. Michael is therefore not only my friend but also my client.'

The sergeant's companion hurriedly flipped over a page of his notebook and scribbled frantically as the sergeant backed off. 'Look,' he said with his hands facing palms outwards as they must have taught him at detective training school. 'No one's accusing anyone. It's routine, that's all.'

Kalazian wasn't impressed. 'If that's the case,' he insisted, 'perhaps I can help both you and my client?'

'I wish you would,' the sergeant muttered and the bristles in his moustache trembled.

'You are trying to establish if there is a connection between this person in the photograph and my client, are you not?'

'Yes.' The sergeant glared at his companion faithfully recording everything.

'And,' said Kalazian, 'if any transaction of a criminal nature took place?'

'Yes.' The sergeant put both hands on the chair in front of him and gripped it for support.

'Well,' said Kalazian and turned to Michael with a reassuring wink, 'apart from your brief encounter outside Uncle's, is there any connection?'

'No,' said Michael.

'Have you got that?' asked Kalazian and the sergeant's

companion nodded. The sergeant turned a strange purple colour.

'And did any transaction of a criminal nature take place?'

Michael thought it might have but with Kalazian in full control said no.

Kalazian turned to the sergeant. 'There you are. And unless you have more to go on than the vague accusations of a spiteful, malicious and bald hamburger man I would advise my client not to answer any more of your questions.'

The sergeant was about to bite Kalazian but thought better of it. He cocked his head at his companion who, with a peculiarly extravagant gesture for a man so fitted to the shadows, finished his notes with a full stop.

'Thank you for your co-operation, gentlemen,' said the sergeant and turned awkwardly as if he wasn't sure he could do it without falling over. His companion followed at a discreet distance with a smirk on his face.

As agile as an orang-utan Kalazian bounded past them and out to the front door which was open ready for their departure. Standing at the kitchen door, Michael heard the sergeant say to his companion, 'There's a connection,' and louder to Kalazian, 'We'll be back.'

Kalazian gave a short bow, saw them through the door and slammed it after them. Flushed with victory, he rubbed his hands together and beamed at Michael. Through the open kitchen door behind him Michael could hear children playing in the garden next door; the girls squealing, the boys shouting arrogant orders at each other like little jodhpured, hands-on-the-hips, junior trainee Nazis. He supposed that all boys are Nazis when they think no one's watching. He was one himself he remembered, for the cruelty of it and the pleasure it took in destruction; a rage of metal and fire unleashed on the world to destroy everything. Cities shattered and burned, the air poisoned with smoke and ash; millions dead. Did such things happen? Is there something insane in every one of us that escapes and does such things and frightens us so much we lock it up until we forget how insane it is and let it out again? And so it goes, world without end, amen. And in the times when we keep it locked up, pacing its cage roaring and stinking, we toss it something, a plucked-out eye, to keep it content for a second or so. The solid ground beneath Michael's feet betrayed itself for the raft it was and the waterlogged wood sank below him.

'Michael.' Kalazian put his hand on his shoulder and shook him. 'Come away from the nightmares. Reality's bad enough.' Somehow or other Kalazian was able to walk on the water which Michael supposed, considering his powers, was hardly surprising. If he could keep him in sight he was sure he wouldn't drown.

'Are you my friend?' he asked and allowed Kalazian to escort him over the waves.

'Of course I am. Haven't I told you that?' Kalazian laughed. He offered Michael two little orange rugby balls and Michael took them. Somehow or other Kalazian produced a glass of water — again hardly surprising considering his powers. Michael swallowed the capsules and thanked him.

'Tell me the truth,' he said.

'Is that what friends do?' asked Kalazian, guiding him to the banister where the waves lapped on the shores of this shallow sea.

'Am I dreaming?' asked Michael.

'Mostly, I fear,' said Kalazian and caught him as he stumbled against the bottom step.

'Did I dream about the police just now?' asked Michael and thought Kalazian must have very long arms to be so far away and still keep a hand on his shoulder.

'No,' said Kalazian. 'They were here and most irritating they were too.'

Michael kept his fingers crossed. 'And the eye on the footpath?'

'That was no dream either.'

Michael's fingers uncrossed and his mind went as clear as a glycerine teardrop but he knew that was only the effect of Kalazian's little rugby balls. They stood together outside Anna's room and Kalazian knocked at the door.

Mrs Kalazian, in an ill-fitting green tunic and white plastic apron spattered with bits of tea-soaked bread, opened the door. 'Michael,' she said, her eyes as soft as corduroy buttons. She took him by the arm. 'Anna will see you now.'

A poor choice of words, Michael thought, considering, but Anna sitting up in bed saw him with both eyes open. He turned towards Kalazian standing preening himself in Anna's full-length bedside mirror.

'This is the dream,' Michael said and Kalazian without looking away from the mirror nodded.

'How are you, Anna?' he put his hand on hers. She wouldn't answer, keeping her lips tight shut. Her eyelids flickered and her eyes darted about as if they were trapped.

'She won't eat or drink,' said Mrs Kalazian from the foot of the bed. 'I can't get anything past her teeth. Perhaps you could try?'

With all the disdain of a slippered sultan, Kalazian found a hair in his nostril and stepping closer to the mirror to scrutinise it, plucked it out with a wince using finger and thumb.

'It's herbal tea.' Mrs Kalazian handed Michael a white mug with Anna's name in red letters on the side. 'Drink it,' she whispered to Anna. 'It's good for you.'

The tea was the colour of copper and smelt of mint and aniseed. Michael put the mug to his lips but Mrs Kalazian, her eyes momentarily startled, put her hand on his arm and reminded him, 'It's for Anna.'

Anna was sitting with her head against the headboard and a tiny pool of sweat glistening in the hollow behind her collarbone. She didn't look at all well. 'Drink it,' he whispered and put the mug to her lips. 'It's good for you.'

Anna opened her mouth and drank. Kalazian surreptitiously put the plucked-out nostril hair in his pocket and glanced across at his wife.

'All of it,' whispered Mrs Kalazian.

'All of it,' murmured Michael.

Anna lifted her hand and held it under the mug, tipping it up until the rim touched her nose.

'Every last drop,' whispered Mrs Kalazian.

'Every last drop,' repeated Michael and took the empty mug from Anna's lips. She closed her eyes and through her half-open mouth her breath smelt of mint and aniseed and acetone and bits of tea-soaked bread.

'How peaceful she looks.' Mrs Kalazian dabbed the corners of Anna's mouth with a piece of pink tissue paper.

'She'll sleep now,' said Kalazian, peering at his nostrils in the mirror as if there might be a secret message hidden up one of them.

'Michael,' he said later as he ushered him away from Anna's bed. 'Your love for Anna does you credit.' He silently edged towards the bedroom door and motioned Michael to join him.

'We,' he said, 'that is, Mrs Kalazian and I, love Anna too. We have done so since the day she arrived here scarred and blistered from the fire outside, but our love is a strange love; not everyone understands it.'

Michael agreed and wanted to shake himself free of the chemicals in Kalazian's capsules and demand to know how Anna had been injured but remembered, in this dream, that she hadn't been injured.

'And you too Michael,' Kalazian said, tucking Michael into bed. 'You also are strange. I want you, if you would.' He opened the drawer of Michael's bedside locker and took out the blank book.

'When you wake up of course,' he went on. 'But if you would.' He placed the book on top of the locker and tapped it lightly.

'A full written confession would help us, that is Mrs Kalazian and me; it would help us enormously.'

Michael assured Kalazian he would help him all he could and with Kalazian's blessing fell asleep, which when he thought of it was an odd thing to do in a dream.

7

During the night — or was it the day? It was hard to tell with the curtains drawn and Kalazian's chemicals slopping about in his brain — Michael was privileged to be given an insight into the nature of the universe. He was so excited he jumped out of bed, naked as it happened, and determined to write the insight down before it escaped. He opened the blank book on top of his locker but found it was full of writing already; some sort of confession, by the look of it. The edges of his insight were starting to fray by the time he found a blank page in the erstwhile blank book. The confession itself looked interesting too; madness, poison and murder tempted him but he resisted. He scribbled on the back of his hand with a ballpoint pen until the ink began to flow then started to write down his insight into the nature of the universe.

The trouble was that when he tried to put it into words it didn't come out right. He had divined the essential oneness of all things but when he wrote that down it looked like a lot of pretentious nonsense so he crossed it out. Everything, absolutely everything without exception, was exactly as it should be. Everything, from the whispering spheres out in the fathomless reaches of space to squashed worms and dogshit on the pavement, was exactly right, perfect. Michael wanted to cross that out too. It was better than the first attempt but it didn't explain his insight.

'Words won't explain it,' said Kalazian and offered Michael a peppermint humbug. 'Words, by their very nature, attempt to break up the universe into manageable bits but the universe isn't like that.' Michael clacked the peppermint humbug around in his mouth and nodded his agreement.

'The universe,' said Kalazian and put the packet of peppermint humbugs back in his pocket, 'resists any attempt to reduce it to component parts because, and here is the essence of your insight, Michael, it hasn't got any component parts.'

Michael was so excited he nearly spat out the peppermint. 'That's right,' he said speaking with his mouth full which his mother or someone like her had told him never to do. 'It is,' he pronounced and left it at that, amazed at his own profundity.

'Precisely.' Kalazian gave the secret, omniscient smile that only Zen masters give.

'It's amazing,' said Michael, flushed with peppermint-humbug-flavoured knowledge.

'Not really. It's the sort of thing that happens to everyone who takes too many little orange rugby balls.'

Michael's mouth dropped open and the sucked-down remnant of his peppermint humbug fell out and on to the floor.

'The effect wears off after a few hours,' said Kalazian. A cat as black as his pullover sniffed at the peppermint humbug, arched its back and glared at Michael with sullen resentment.

'It was a mystical not a chemical experience,' said Michael, but the cat turned its stuck-on button bottom at him and flicked its tail.

'Mystical, chemical,' Kalazian chuckled. 'It's all the same. I've had dozens of them.' The cat, prowling around Kalazian's feet, stuck its nose in the turned-up cuff of his trousers and sneezed. He picked it up and brushed the fluff off its nose.

'But where has it got me?' Kalazian continued, raising his voice to make himself heard above the cat's purring. 'I haven't turned into a Bodhisattva. I still eat, I still scratch, I still fart and so for that matter do Bodhisattvas; it's just that nobody mentions it.' He chuckled again and the cat purred louder and nuzzled into the crook of his arm.

Michael longed to wrap himself up in a warm and woolly discussion about Bodhisattvas. During his travels he'd met a number of enlightened beings and when he thought of it they ate and scratched and farted too.

'No, Michael,' Kalazian said. 'It's the chemicals. Sit down. Wait until they wear off.'

So he sat down and waited in Kalazian's own armchair; a privilege, he thought, though the chair was infested with cat fleas. After the chemicals had worn off and the three fleas on the back of his hand swelled up and turned black with blood, Kalazian brought Michael a bowl of peppery tomato soup.

'How,' said Michael and stirred his soup with Kalazian's own silver soup spoon, 'how's Anna now?' He pictured Mrs Kalazian, kind and simple as a nun, sponging Anna's arms and combing her hair. He was glad all the business about the eye was only a nightmare and savoured the taste of the peppery soup.

'Don't worry,' said Kalazian. 'She's quite dead.'

Michael dropped his spoon. Kalazian picked it off the table and put it back in his hand but he dropped it again.

'Mrs Kalazian is laying her out right now,' said Kalazian. 'Sponging her arms and combing her hair. It was an act of great kindness you did for Anna, Michael. We, that is Mrs Kalazian and I, are proud of you and grateful. We, though we loved her almost as much as you, could never have done it.'

Michael looked at his watch as he picked up the spoon and bent his head closer to the soup bowl. It was 9.20, a.m. or p.m.? There was light coming through the kitchen window and the giggles and screams of children playing in the next-door neighbour's garden. If he ate the soup quickly enough he would have time to catch the 9.30 bus into Auckland, then the Railways bus down to Wellington; spend the night there, maybe go to a movie and then on to an Italian restaurant; why not, he was on holiday? The next day he would catch the Picton ferry. The crossing would be just the thing to clear his head. From Picton down to Greymouth and from there work his way down the West Coast to the beech forests, rivers and mountains of Fiordland. He would be free there in the dripping green forests. Among the moss-covered rocks and the caterpillars and spiders, centipedes and snails, he would be free. He was tempted to drink the soup straight from the bowl but out of politeness used Kalazian's silver spoon; not too polite however to spoon in the soup one mouthful after the other without stopping.

'Careful, careful,' said Kalazian. 'You'll choke.'

Michael forgot about politeness. It was 9.22. He lifted the soup bowl and drank the last drop. 'I've a bus to catch,' he said and pushed the soup bowl across the table.

'You've a body to bury,' said Kalazian.

So Anna was dead. Poisoned, they said. And her right eye was missing so it hadn't been a dream; unless of course this was the dream. Michael seemed to be slipping in and out of them so easily lately. It looked like a dream, blurred and glistening.

'She looks so peaceful,' said Kalazian. He gave Michael a large white handkerchief with a K embroidered so prettily in one corner. Michael wiped his eyes and sniffed. 'Mrs Kalazian's done a lovely job.'

'She's had practice,' said Kalazian.

Knowing Kalazian would insist he keep it, Michael put the handkerchief in his coat pocket.

'When she was only fourteen,' said Kalazian, 'she laid out her father and mother, three sisters and a brother in a single night all in a row clean and tidy for when the ambulance called the following morning.'

'I didn't know that,' said Michael. There was a trace of a smile on Anna's lips and he wondered if it was Mrs Kalazian's art or the true expression on Anna's face when she died.

'It was before your time,' said Kalazian. 'Though quite a sensation in its day.'

'What killed them?' asked Michael and Kalazian answered, 'Kindness.'

'They were suffering?'

'Ah, Michael,' Kalazian's bottom lip quivered and there were tears in his eyes. 'I knew you'd understand. So few people did then, or now. In their ignorance they locked Mrs Kalazian away for years.'

'It's a terrible thing,' said Michael, 'to be locked away.'

'It is.' Kalazian dabbed at his eyes with another large white monogrammed handkerchief. 'In a more enlightened society Mrs Kalazian's action, or Jenny Margolis as she was then, would have been recognised for its compassion and humanity.' He gestured to Michael to lift Anna's legs while he lifted her shoulders and, gently so as not to break her, they placed her on the canvas stretcher on the floor at the side of the bed.

'As it was,' he went on, puffing already from the exertion,

'people reviled her as a monster, a criminal. They looked at her, in their ignorance, with fear and horror.'

'People don't understand,' said Michael and with a nod from Kalazian lifted the stretcher.

'It's true, I'm afraid.' The tree outside Anna's window tapped at the glass with its skeleton fingers. 'They didn't understand her and they wouldn't, if ever they found out, understand you. They might, indeed they probably would, lock you away.'

'But I've done nothing wrong.' Michael lifted the stretcher to shoulder height to keep it level as he descended the stairs. Kalazian, puffing and grunting at the other end of the stretcher, didn't reply.

Outside in the back garden it was dark, so Michael would have been too late for the 9.30 bus even if he had left as soon as he'd finished his soup. Anyway, he had no intention of leaving now. Certain that Kalazian would protect him he placed himself entirely in his hands. It started to drizzle and the sodium lights strung out on the roads leading into the city were reflected in a faint orange glow on the underside of the clouds. Kalazian sprinkled half a sackful of quicklime over Anna's body where it lay a metre down in the clay.

'Hurry,' he said and Michael's arms already aching from digging the hole earlier that day ached even more as he shovelled the piled-up dirt on to Anna's body. When he had nearly filled the hole Kalazian with his hair stuck down on his forehead from the drizzle placed two rose bushes in the ground.

'By way of remembrance,' he said.

Michael had to wipe his eyes with the monogrammed handkerchief before he finished shovelling. He trod down the dirt with the two-sizes-too-big gumboots kindly lent to him by Kalazian, and noticed Mr Charles looking down at him from behind the curtain of his bedroom window.

Mrs Kalazian, not at all like a monster or criminal, had a hot cup of tea waiting for them both when they came in from the garden.

'Drink up quickly,' she said, but Michael smelt it first and took only a tiny sip.

Kalazian patted him heartily on the shoulder. 'What's the matter, Michael,' he said, 'don't you trust us?'

'Not entirely.' Michael drank the tea but he didn't die. Mrs Kalazian as kind as a buttered crumpet sat down next to him and took his hand in both of hers.

'Michael,' she said and stroked his hand. He had never noticed before, but she smelt of chocolate-coated caramel and popcorn. Perhaps that's what she ate to keep up her strength in the face of living with Kalazian and helping him murder people?

'You're not a murderer,' she said. 'No more than I was when I was fourteen years old.'

'It's true, Michael,' said Kalazian and flicked through the notes in his wallet. 'You haven't murdered anyone.'

Michael felt a sudden flash of reality, or what seemed like reality. It lasted long enough for him to say, and very firmly too, 'I know I haven't, you have.' He pulled his hand away from Mrs Kalazian but she took it back. Her hands felt so warm and safe that he let her keep it. He felt sure she or Kalazian — it didn't matter which — would explain everything to him.

'Think, Michael,' said Mrs Kalazian. 'Who gave her the tea?'

'I didn't know it was poisoned.'

'Didn't you?' Mrs Kalazian wasn't trying to trap him or trick him or trip him up. She only wanted him to see the truth. He knew that.

'Don't be frightened of Mrs Kalazian, Michael,' said Kalazian. 'She has strange powers but she only wants you to see the truth. You know that.' He took two twenty-dollar notes out of his wallet and put them in Michael's top pocket.

'Take my car,' he said. 'Here's the keys.' He put them on the table in front of Michael. 'Get a flagon of semillon from Henty's, cold mind you.' He frowned to emphasise the last point. 'And three doner kebabs with the trimmings from the Middle Eastern. You know where it is?'

'Yes,' said Michael and pushed the two twenty-dollar notes

more securely into his pocket. 'Through the lights past Henty's and halfway down the hill.'

In no more time than it takes to drive to Henty's and the Middle Eastern and back Michael returned with doner kebabs still hot and the semillon still cold. 'And delicious they are too,' pronounced Kalazian wiping his mouth with a piece of kitchen paper towel. Michael and Mrs Kalazian both on their last mouthful nodded in agreement while Kalazian topped up their wine glasses. Mrs Kalazian resumed her seat next to Michael and took his hand again.

'It was my father who killed them,' she said. 'He spared me to do the tidying up.'

'A neat and meticulous man, Mr Margolis,' Kalazian added and settled back in his armchair to enjoy the story. 'I admired him greatly.'

'If your father killed them, why did you get locked away?' asked Michael. It seemed a simple enough question.

'A simple enough question,' Kalazian agreed.

'And simply answered.' Mrs Kalazian leant closer to Michael, allowing him to breathe in the smell of popcorn and semillon and caramel and doner kebab. 'I was the instrument of his wishes. He made the poison. I gave it.'

'Poison is the kindest way,' said Kalazian, picking a dead moth out of his wine. 'If you know what you're doing.'

'He put the poison in their tea,' said Mrs Kalazian, 'and never said a word to me. He didn't have to.'

'They were a very close family,' murmured Kalazian.

'I gave the tea to my father, my mother, two sisters and brother and in no time at all they were dead.'

Mrs Kalazian stroked Michael's hand. Tears gathered on the rims of her lower eyelids and overflowed. Mr Kalazian produced yet another large white monogrammed handkerchief and gave it to his wife.

'It was a beautiful sight,' said Mrs Kalazian and sniffed. 'They looked so peaceful.' She paused to dry her eyes and blow her nose. 'They suffered so much in life. I was glad to be the instrument of their deaths.'

'What did they suffer from?' asked Michael and Kalazian gave him a slow wink to indicate his approval of the question. His wife however had taken to weeping again so Kalazian, confident as ever, took over.

'Insanity,' he said and Michael coughed to remind himself he had once suffered from consumption and nothing else. 'Margolis, through no fault of his own I hasten to add, had tainted them all with his madness and being mad.' He shook his head slowly. 'They suffered.'

'Mrs Kalazian too; I mean Jenny Margolis as she was then?' asked Michael and Mrs Kalazian squeezed his hand in affection.

'Her worst of all,' said Kalazian. 'Not because she was insane then or now or any other time but because she was sane. Her father, a perceptive as well as neat and meticulous man, recognised this. Of course he never said as much.'

'He didn't have to,' Mrs Kalazian's voice came through the handkerchief held up to her nose. 'We were a very close family.'

Outside the drizzle had turned to rain and pattered on the iron roof. Michael wondered if Anna felt cold out there in the garden and thought perhaps he and Kalazian should have wrapped her up in something warmer than a winding sheet.

'Mr Margolis,' Kalazian continued and poured himself another glass of wine, 'knew that Jenny understood his suffering and the suffering of his wife and children. He knew he could rely on her to give them the poison. Besides . . .' he flicked at the drops of wine on the tips of his moustache, 'he knew they trusted her and didn't trust him. They thought he was insane and would never have taken tea from him.'

'In case it poisoned them?' said Michael.

'Exactly.'

'Exactly,' echoed Kalazian's wife.

'I see,' said Michael. He could smell the garlic from the doner kebab on his fingertips as he stroked his lips in an effort to coax the right words out from the crowd that had gathered in his mouth.

'Why,' he whispered to Mrs Kalazian, 'if you were suffering too, didn't you take the poison?'

With his ear cocked and listening, Kalazian answered for his sobbing wife. 'Mrs Kalazian suffered and continues to suffer yet she doesn't take poison because, Michael,' he breathed his semilloned breath past Michael's ear, 'she is a saint.'

'A saint?' Michael wondered if Kalazian was right; he so often was.

Mrs Kalazian blushed behind her monogrammed handkerchief.

'Yes,' said Kalazian. 'A saint no less; the same as you, Michael, and let's have no false modesty . . .' He lowered his eyelids slowly over his big brown gobstopper eyes. 'The same as I am a saint.'

Michael understood perfectly. 'She stays alive in spite of her suffering,' he said, 'to alleviate the suffering of others?'

'Exactly.'

'Exactly,' his wife sniffed.

'How many Annas have there been?' asked Michael.

Kalazian furrowed his brow and stared up at the far corner of the kitchen ceiling. 'Including the most recent one,' he said, tapping the tip of each finger with the index finger of the opposite hand, 'eight in all.'

'And how many Michaels?' whispered Michael.

'Eight,' Kalazian was much quicker to answer. 'One for each. But none as good as you. He's the best, isn't he?' He stroked a lock of hair away from his wife's eye.

'Yes,' Mrs Kalazian leaned towards Michael and kissed him on the cheek. 'The best.'

'They were all saints too?' said Michael.

'Every one,' said Kalazian.

'Every one,' agreed his wife, caressing Michael's arm.

'What happened to the other saints?'

'Gone.' Firmly but gently he took Mrs Kalazian's hand from Michael's arm. 'One way or another. One I believe is living in the dripping forests of Fiordland among the moss-covered rocks and fallen trees,' he added, almost as an afterthought.

8

Mallis apparently didn't think Michael was a saint. The following morning when Michael was in the bathroom writing Mallis's name on the steamed-up mirror, Mallis tried to murder him. He had naturally chosen for his weapon the kukri. One cut from that delivered with force from a practised arm would have taken Michael's head off in no more time than it takes to lop the top off a carrot. Fortunately or not, Mallis was wildly erratic in his aim. He missed Michael and sliced the plastic shower curtain down the middle instead. Michael could see that Mallis was upset and rather than speak to him there and then decided to escape from the bathroom, in spite of the fact he was wrapped only in a bath towel, while Mallis slashed and thrashed about in the remains of the shower curtain.

Unfortunately or not, Mallis had locked the bathroom door and taken the key out of the lock. Michael, naturally, was desperate. In the confined space of the bathroom, even if Mallis continued to slash erratically, he was bound to hit Michael sooner or later. His hair slicked down, moustache neatly trimmed for a change and wearing a black gaberdine overcoat of post-war vintage, Mallis, however, reassured him.

'Don't worry,' he said picking bits of shower curtain off the kukri before sheathing it. 'I've changed my mind.'

Michael had slipped on the wet floor and half fallen against the wall. He held on to the sink conveniently placed nearby, and was using it as a support to raise himself. Mallis kicked his legs from under him and Michael fell, hitting his head against the wall.

'Unlike you,' said Mallis and took the bathroom door key from his overcoat pocket, 'I take my pleasures among the living.' He unlocked the door, gave Michael another kick and closed the door quietly as he left.

Mrs Kalazian put Hirudoid ointment on Michael's bruises. She reminded him very much of Anna, the way she tended him, and for some reason Michael couldn't understand, his eyes filled with tears. He pulled up his underpants and trousers and fastened the buckle on his belt. Kalazian gave him a handkerchief — he seemed to have an endless supply — and said, 'It's true. Mallis does take his pleasures among the living. Only the living feel pain.' He puffed up his chest and was about to give his observations on the psychology of Mallis when Mallis himself, in no mood for observations psychological or otherwise, stalked into the kitchen and demanded an audience. With his hands deep in his black gaberdine overcoat pockets he glared at Kalazian.

'Kalazian,' he said. 'I thought we had an agreement.'

Michael shuffled around to the safe side of the table, out of range of Mallis's boots.

'Henry,' Kalazian began and spread his arms as benovolent as ever, but Mallis wasn't having it.

'At least two months,' he said. 'That was our contract.'

Kalazian shrugged with a gesture that could have dismissed every calamity that has befallen the human race since its first shrew-like ancestors shuddered in the shadow of the dinosaurs. 'Circumstances changed,' he said.

'What use,' said Mallis between his teeth, 'is a dead body to me? I might be a pervert, but I'm not a necrophiliac.'

Mrs Kalazian, a source of comfort and strength in an emergency, switched on the electric kettle and picked out, from a selection of Twinings tea caddies, the Lapsang Souchong.

'Henry,' Kalazian continued in his conciliatory tone, 'I know under your passionate exterior you are a reasonable man.'

Mallis picked up a bone china plate, reached across the table and broke the plate over Michael's head. 'Is that the action of a reasonable man?' he asked. With her back to Mallis, Mrs Kalazian closed her eyes and with her mouth shut tight breathed heavily through her nose.

Kalazian tutted. 'Bone china,' he said. 'I think you might have made your point equally well with a less expensive piece of crockery. This piece, for instance,' he picked up a plain white bread-and-butter plate with a chip out of the side. Mallis snatched it from his hand and placed it gently back on the table.

Still dazed from Mallis's assault in the bathroom, rugby balls and murder, Michael was on the verge of passing out. His head fell forward, sprinkling bits of porcelain on the tabletop. Mrs Kalazian was at his side before his forehead hit the table but it was no use. Though she helped him to sit back in the chair, Michael's head might as well have stayed on the table and had an entire fifty-piece Royal Doulton dinner set broken over it, one at a time, for all the good its contents were. Kalazian's voice came to him from the end of the tunnel.

'I think,' Kalazian said, 'Michael better take the day off. The strain's too much for him.'

He had a wonderful time with Anna that afternoon. It was a clear, crisp, clean and bright winter's day. He took her to Karekare beach in Kalazian's car. There was nobody there but themselves. Mrs Kalazian, kind as a bacon sandwich fresh from the frying pan, had packed them a picnic lunch. There was french bread, smoked chicken, lettuce, tomato and mayonnaise. There was cold Lambrusca and for afters a slice of homemade fruit cake with marzipan topping followed by Nicaraguan coffee hot from a thermos flask. The whole scene was a bit blurred and fuzzy and Anna never opened her eyes once, but apart from that everything was perfect.

Anna stroked his hand and kissed the small white scar left from the cut of the kukri. It seemed such a long time since that happened; two or three hundred years at least. She laughed when he told her this and said something in a foreign language, French or Russian; she said it so softly it was hard to tell. When he leaned closer the better to hear her, the roar of the sea took her words away. If only she'd open her eyes, perhaps he could have understood what she was trying to say but she kept them closed.

And there was another strange thing. Even though he could hear her voice and her laughter, her mouth didn't move. They hid in the sand dunes from the sea and the wind. For the fun of it Michael buried Anna up to her neck in sand and for the hell of it buried her head as well. He just had time to plant two rose bushes on top of her before the fuzziness at the edge of the scene closed in and Mallis tapped him on the shoulder and accused him of being a murderer. Michael shrugged him off and Mallis whisked out of sight like a magician's handkerchief but it was no good; he knew he was dreaming. If he didn't hurry before he woke up he would lose Anna for ever.

What a stupid game to play, burying her in the sand. The rose bush markers had gone but she couldn't be far away. He dug in the sand and the sand, being sand, poured back into the hole as quickly as he dug it out. From under his half-open eyelids he could see Kalazian waiting in a rocking chair with a fire in the grate behind him and a mantelpiece and mirror above his head.

'Ah Michael,' he said as Michael with his eyes tight shut ran around the sand dunes looking for the right spot to dig. 'You're awake at last. We, that is Mrs Kalazian and I, were becoming quite concerned.'

Michael kept his eyes shut but Kalazian insisted.

'The trouble with reality, Michael, is that it won't go away.'

He opened his eyes to hear Kalazian's observations.

'Reality,' said Kalazian with the tips of his fingers together to form an arch, 'is like a dog; a badly behaved dog; always snapping at your heels, demanding to be noticed. You know what dogs are like?'

Michael had had a dog many years ago. Its name was Curmudgeon and it bit everything including the hand that fed it. Michael, naturally, loved it, but when it bit the pretty little golden-haired girl next door and dirtied her party dress he had to have Curmudgeon put down; the community in its wisdom and outrage said so.

'Yes, I know what dogs are like,' he said.

'You can hide from a dog, in your room if you like,' said Kalazian as if he knew nothing of Michael's love for the lost Curmudgeon, 'but when you come out, and you always have to come out, what do you find?' He threw his arms up in dismay at the destruction before him. 'It's torn the place apart and crapped everywhere. Reality's like that, Michael; destructive and smelly if you take your eyes off it for too long.'

Michael sat up in the couch and felt the top of his head. There was a lump where Mallis had broken the plate. He pressed it as hard as he could until the pain woke him up. Kalazian rubbed his hands together in approval.

'Excellent,' he said. 'Pain is the most potent reminder of reality. Press the top of your head whenever you feel yourself slipping away, Michael.' He sat back in the rocking chair with a smile of satisfaction.

'There are times,' he went on, 'when I could do with a lump like that but not now.'

He stood up suddenly and left the rocking chair rocking. Michael thought it stayed rocking too long; as if someone was still in it. He pressed the top of his head.

'Keep pressing, Michael.' Kalazian paced up and down in front of the fire. 'Mr Charles has been arrested.'

Michael didn't care a fig or any other kind of laxative for Mr Charles but Kalazian looked concerned so out of politeness he said, 'How terrible,' and tried to look equally dismayed.

'Ordinarily,' said Kalazian, 'I wouldn't care a fig for Mr Charles. He took risks; he knew that he took them. Things have come out against him, that's all.' He stopped pacing and stood on tiptoe with his back to the fire. Michael wondered that Kalazian's feet didn't buckle under the strain but also knew he was remarkably well co-ordinated and could have turned a pirouette if he'd wanted. He was disappointed when Kalazian didn't take up the idea but began pacing again.

'What worries me,' said Kalazian, 'is what Mr Charles might say under duress. He's a terrible chatterbox you know.'

Michael remembered Mr Charles at the window. Though he had done nothing he was ashamed of, he knew, as in the case of Mrs Kalazian, that no one would understand. He realised however that Kalazian had a plan and was eager to help in any way he could.

'What was he arrested for?' he asked.

'Importuning young boys.' Kalazian tutted his disapproval, not for the importuning but because Mr Charles had been indiscreet. 'He must be losing his touch.' He stood on tiptoe again. 'He usually has such a good eye for the cynical young thugs he brings back here to beat him up and rob him.'

'That's terrible,' said Michael before he could stop himself.

'It's not terrible,' said Kalazian but there was no reproach in his voice. He was merely stating a fact. 'It's what he likes. Sometimes he even has the delights of fellatio and on rare occasions sodomy, so generally there's no harm done and no complaints, but as I say,' he dropped his shoulders and sighed, 'he must be losing his touch. This time one of the boys laid an official complaint with the police. While you were dreaming of picnics at the beach the police arrested him.'

'I'm sorry,' said Michael though he didn't care a fig for Mr Charles.

'I don't care a fig or any kind of laxative for Mr Charles,' said Kalazian. 'I do however care for myself and Mrs Kalazian and more particularly, for you, Michael.'

He was kind and compassionate as always. Michael could hear the police sirens wailing after their prey down in the gully and the rose leaves tapping against each other in the wind. His eyes started to mist up. Kalazian walked across to him with the purposeful stride of a paperback hero and pressed the top of his head.

Wide awake, Michael asked, 'What's the plan?'

The plan was simple. Michael was to present himself at the police station as a friend of Mr Charles and post bail for him. The charge was not a major one so bail should not present a problem or be too expensive for that matter.

'It's as well,' Kalazian had said, 'that importuning was as far as Mr Charles got. Any mention of sodomy and the police would have their truncheons out quicker than you could say petroleum jelly.'

Mr Charles laughed through his tears of gratitude when Michael told him that. 'Oh Edward's such a wag,' he said, 'and so kind and compassionate.' His eyes nearly washed out of their sockets with all the tears that poured from them. Fortunately

Michael had been given a supply of Kalazian's big white handerchiefs. 'You're sure to need them,' Kalazian had said.

Mr Charles buried his face in the handkerchief and held Michael's hand. The desk sergeant, twice as large as her desk, tried to frown her disapproval but her hair was pulled back so tight she had to be content with pursing her lips.

'Sign here,' she said and swivelled a big black book around on the desk. She gave Mr Charles his belt, his watch, and three gaudy rings in a plastic bag. Mr Charles didn't check them. A tear dripped off the end of his nose and landed on the book.

'I'm sorry, I'm sorry,' he pleaded and tried to wipe it away but ended up smearing his own and several other signatures. The sergeant snatched the book back, glowered at it and slammed it shut.

Behind her was a map of Auckland covered with stars and numbers and coloured dots. Michael tried to pick out Kalazian's boarding house and thought he could see it behind the sergeant's right ear.

'You can go now,' she said with her shoulders straight and her chest pushed out. When neither Michael nor Mr Charles moved she slapped her hand down on the desk and said, 'Both of you.'

A narrow corridor led to the outside door. It was dimly lit but Michael recognised the bristly moustache of the sergeant who had interviewed him — when was it? A couple of days or a couple of decades ago? Mr Charles twisted around trying to get his belt through the loops as Michael hurried him on ahead and nodded at the sergeant who didn't return the nod but grinned and said, 'We meet again.'

It was an innocent remark but Michael knew there was no escape. His position was hopeless. His heart and his brain were wrapped in cellophane and thrown in the freezer with the date stamped on them. A wonderful sense of despair settled over him. It was only a matter of time before his crime, for such it would seem to those who didn't understand, would be exposed. He was clearing his throat ready to give a full confession when Mr Charles pulled the elbow of his coat.

'Please Michael,' he said, 'I can't bear to spend another second in this awful place.'

The sergeant, still grinning, stepped briskly down the corridor and held the door wide open, flattening himself against the wall. 'You must call again,' he said and Michael heard him laugh as he slammed the door behind them.

Michael wondered if, in the interests of safety, he shouldn't give Mr Charles a cup of Kalazian's tea immediately they returned to the boarding house. His passenger wriggled luxuriously into his seat and clicked the seat belt shut before reaching up to the rear-vision mirror and peering at himself.

'Oh my God,' he said, quickly smoothing his eyebrows with a wet finger, 'I look an absolute fright.'

Michael readjusted the mirror.

'You've no idea what it's like,' said Mr Charles, looking eagerly out of the side window as if he was five years old and off to the circus. 'Those awful little cells. They smell like public conveniences.' He pulled a face and shuddered.

Michael decided as he drove along Hobson Street that it wouldn't be very sensible to give Mr Charles a cup of tea immediately. The best thing would be to wait a few days. If Mr Charles had talked, the police would be around within a day at the most. Give him the tea too soon and there'd be two bodies to explain instead of one.

Still, once you start there's no stopping. Mr Charles would have to go sooner or later, and Mallis too. Mallis wouldn't talk but a man capable of hitting you over the head with expensive porcelain is capable of anything. Mallis would be difficult, though. He was far too paranoid to drink tea. A clout over the back of the head with a shovel when he wasn't looking; something like that would probably be best. And why stop there? The Kalazians, kind and compassionate as they were, might, with three murders on their hands, turn Queen's evidence, whatever that was, unless of course Elizabeth took the advice of the women's magazines and retired in favour of her son in which case it would be King's evidence. Either way, the back garden was big enough for both of them and a bristly moustachioed detective if he came around with his grinning innuendos. How dare he even suggest that Michael had never suffered from consumption, had never been in hospital, had never been to the city of Baktapur and seen that evil little statue smeared with ghee and spattered with betel juice and chicken blood!

'My, my.' Mr Charles jumped up and down in his seat and looked quickly over his shoulder. 'Are you all right, Michael? You just went through a red light.'

Michael pulled over to the side of the road and took a deep breath. 'I'm sorry,' he said. 'My mind's been playing tricks lately.'

'My advice to you,' said Mr Charles, 'is don't drink Edward's tea. He puts things in it. You wouldn't catch me drinking it. Oh no.' He winked at Michael. 'Oh no.'

Kalazian, with a smile as wide as a halloween pumpkin, had a surly, pouting, tight-jeaned young man waiting for Mr Charles when he returned. 'It wouldn't surprise me,' he said to Michael as Mr Charles went upstairs with his present, 'if that young man beat Mr Charles within an inch of his life.'

'What about that last inch?' Michael asked, eager to please. But Kalazian, clever as ever, laughed and said, 'There's plenty of time. His trial, if there is one, won't come up for weeks yet.'

Michael was sorely tried later that evening in the laundry. When he wasn't watching, Mallis tried to clout him over the back of the head with a coal shovel. Fortunately or not, Mallis's aim was as erratic this time as it was when he tried to slice Michael in half with the kukri. A glancing blow above the ear was all Michael received. It was enough to shave off a clump of hair and tip him face forward into the washing basket but no more.

The shovel struck the washing machine, which clanged like a gong, sprung open the front loading door and dowsed Michael with hot soapy water full of whiteners, brighteners, enzymes and deodorants. Michael was, naturally, dazed and Mallis, if he'd wanted to, could have finished him off with a few more belts from the coal shovel. Fortunately or not, Mallis threw the shovel with a clatter to the concrete floor, sat down in the tubular steel chair designed for the watching of the washing through the glass in the door of the front-loader, and handed Michael a dry towel.

Michael dried his hair, gingerly avoiding the scalped area, and sat down in another tubular steel chair to listen to Mallis's explanation. Mallis took out an apricot energy food bar from the pocket of his black overcoat and offered it to Michael, who shook his head. 'To be honest,' he said, 'I'm feeling a bit sick.'

Mallis shrugged. 'Hardly surprising, I suppose.' He unwrapped the cellophane wrapper and bit the end off the energy bar. 'You might find this difficult to believe,' he chewed contemplatively, 'but I'm your friend.'

Through the ceiling directly above their heads but from the room above the room above, came screams. It was probably only Mr Charles being beaten up so neither Michael nor Mallis paid them much attention.

'I can believe it,' Michael said and he could. His head felt so hollow he was capable of believing anything. Mallis bit off another piece of apricot energy bar and chewed it with his mouth open. The screams through the ceiling grew fainter. He popped the last of the energy bar into his mouth, gave it two chews and swallowed it.

'Why,' he said, 'do you think I've tried to kill you, how many times is it now?' He frowned, looked up towards the right of his frontal lobe where he kept his pocket calculator, closed his eyes, opened them and said, 'Three times.'

'That's right.' Michael had worked it out before Mallis.

'Well, why is it?'

Michael thought it was as plain as the nose on his face. 'Hatred, jealousy, anger, revenge, frustration.'

'As plain as the nose on your face?' asked Mallis.

'Yes.'

'Nothing so plain,' said Mallis. He leaned forward and smiled an apricot-scented smile at Michael. 'I did it for love,' he said.

Michael could understand. The love Mallis felt for Anna was

so polluted with hatred and anger that without her to take them on herself they would be turned on the person who took her away.

'Jesus,' said Mallis, 'you're so bloody naïve.' He leaned so close to Michael that the nose on his face was plain to see with all its pores and broken blood vessels and little black hairs growing from the tip. 'I didn't love Anna,' he said. 'I never loved her. It's you I love, Michael. Don't you understand that?'

Michael could understand but he also understood that in his current state of mind he was capable of understanding anything from obscure Armenian dialects to the fact that a man who claimed to love him had tried to kill him three times. When Mallis arose and undid the big black buttons on his overcoat he wasn't alarmed. He knew there was nothing physical in Mallis's love.

'Don't be alarmed,' said Mallis. 'There's nothing physical in my love for you.' He undid the buckle on his trouser belt, let it out a notch and did it up again.

'It's amazing,' he went on, 'how an apricot energy bar makes you swell.'

'Will you try to kill me again?' asked Michael.

'No,' said Mallis and beneath his black moustache the corners of his mouth turned down. 'I wish I could,' he added, 'but I'm not like you. I can't kill for love.' He sighed and did up the buttons on his overcoat. 'When whatever happens to you happens, I hope you can find it in your heart to forgive me.'

He held out his hand to Michael and as Michael shook it he thought he saw a teardrop glistening in the right-hand corner of Mallis's right-hand eye, but in his current state of mind he could have been mistaken.

9

All the charges against Mr Charles were dropped. The police gave no explanation other than the fact that the complaints against Mr Charles had been withdrawn. Mr Charles surmised that the young boy he had importuned, and he had never denied, except to the police, that he had importuned him, had had what Mr Charles termed 'an awakening'. 'I opened the door to his closet,' he explained. 'The poor dear delicious boy pulled it shut again but sitting there in the dark he's had time to think. He's probably opened the closet all by himself now and wonders where I've gone.' He finished his analysis by blaming the whole embarrassing episode on the parents. Whether his explanation was correct or not, Mr Charles was so happy he had decided to have a small celebration. The small celebration had, however, turned out to be a big one. His room was packed full of people and smoke and noise.

'I didn't want to offend anyone,' he explained, pushing his way through the crowd to give Michael a glass of champagne. 'Dom Perignon. For my very special friends.'

Apart from a slight red scar above his upper lip there was nothing about Mr Charles's appearance to suggest that only ten or eleven days ago he had been beaten within an inch of his life. Michael thought he recognised the surly-faced boy who had done it over by the window with a canapé in his hand pretending to listen to a red-faced broken-nosed rugby player but scowling all the while at the back of Mr Charles's head.

'Ooh,' Mr Charles pouted and narrowed his eyes. 'I better get back to him. He's so moody.' He blew Michael a kiss and with his arms above his head like a Balinese temple dancer wriggled his way through the crowd to his erstwhile assailant. In a rush of generosity with the champagne bubbles prickling his nose, Michael felt happy for Mr Charles. A simple man with simple needs, content with a place to stay, champagne to drink, a boy in his bed and a bruise or two.

Kalazian, surrounded by admirers all at least a head shorter than himself — and those who weren't bowed to make themselves so — held court by the table with the chips and the French onion dip. One of his admirers stayed close by his shoulder. She had white fingers as pale as porcelain and nibbled at a chip as if she intended to make it last all night. She was dressed in black, her cheeks were hollow, her eyes were sunken, her lips were red; she was the bride of Dracula. Michael thought it wouldn't take much poison to finish her off. Kalazian had a glass of red wine in his hand and was listening with great patience to an argument, doubtless on the meaning of life, from a young man with a wispy beard and glasses as thick as milk bottle bottoms. Michael glanced around the room quickly to see if Mrs Kalazian or Mallis was there. Neither of them was but the detective sergeant with the bristly moustache, in the shadows behind Kalazian, raised a half-full glass of champagne to Michael and drank his health.

There was a crash of glass and a loud scream from Mr Charles's bedroom. Through the open door Michael could see a broad-shouldered man in an ill-fitting green frock. He had a broken bottle in one hand and the terrified remnants of a much better dressed transvestite in the other. The hum and chatter of the party died down and above it the man shouted. 'We can't all afford cerise evening gowns.'

Mr Charles with both hands to his cheeks ran to the rescue. 'Oh my God,' he called. 'Someone's insulted Calpurnia.'

The bride of Dracula clung closer to Kalazian as Mr Charles rushed past. Kalazian roared with laughter which was the signal for the hum and chatter to start again.

The sergeant, if he'd ever been there to begin with, had now mercifully vanished. Michael finished his champagne and while Mr Charles soothed the now-sobbing Calpurnia, decided to join Kalazian's admirers. Before he could move, his empty glass was steadied in his hand and the sergeant filled it with champagne from a black and gold bottle. 'Some party eh?' he chuckled.

Michael gulped down too big a mouthful of champagne and coughed till his eyes watered. 'Down the wrong hole eh?' the sergeant said. 'There's a lot of that sort of thing around here.' He chuckled again.

A plate of sausage rolls tried to scurry past Michael's elbow but he caught one before it escaped. It was delicious; the pastry light and flaky and the meat spicy. He licked a piece of pastry off his lower lip and smiled, he hoped not too nervously, at the sergeant. 'Official visit?' he asked, craning his neck around the sergeant to see if anyone was taking notes. No one was.

The sergeant put his full champagne glass on the table next to him and handed Michael a card from inside his inside pocket. 'In a way,' he said.

The card was an invitation edged in gold. 'An invitation is Extended to a Representative of Her Majesty's New Zealand Police Force to Attend a Small Party,' it said. 'To be given by Mr G. Charles at his Residence. Flat 3 No. 27 Kingsland Terrace, Kingsland. 7-7.30 p.m. This Saturday.' It was written in Kalazian's copperplate.

'A joke,' the sergeant said. 'But,' he added, taking the card off Michael and returning it to his pocket, 'I like a bit of a laugh. Ha, ha, ha.' Michael felt the dread of someone about to be asked what was buried in the garden.

Amidst the hubbub and chatter and clatter the sergeant's voice was as crisp as a hot buttered crumpet. 'Your young Maori friend,' he said, 'the one outside Uncle's,' though Michael knew well who he meant. 'You know,' said the sergeant peering expertly for evidence at the end of the sausage roll in his hand, 'the one you didn't know.'

'Yes,' said Michael and hoped the sergeant wouldn't take too much offence at the annoyance in his voice; a little offence but not too much.

'Well,' said the sergeant, brightly as if he hadn't taken any offence at all. 'You know.' He coughed and laughed and bit the end off his sausage roll. 'Well you don't know, do you?'

His eyes twinkled in merriment at the pleasures of his chosen profession. 'He nearly killed four young hoons,' he said, speaking with his mouth full. 'No great loss, you might say, but the law is the law. Set fire to their car.' He picked up his champagne glass and washed down the chewed-up sausage roll without stopping to take a breath. 'Aahh,' he said and smacked his lips. 'Lovely stuff.'

He filled the glass again and topped up Michael's. Mr Charles with his young assailant on one side and the now fully recovered Calpurnia on the other waved from across the room. The sergeant waved back. 'Silly old sodomite,' he laughed and in the same jocular tone said, 'The hoons, more's the pity, escaped with a slight scorching but the car went up with a lovely bang.'

'You saw it?' asked Michael, sorry he'd missed it.

'No,' said the sergeant, 'but your young Maori friend gave a beautiful description. He had me in stitches.' He looked to the left and right, narrowed his eyes and lowered his voice. 'The strange thing is,' he said, 'he did it for you.'

Kalazian appeared out of the murk with his bride clinging to his arm, her lips twitching. 'Sergeant,' he said. 'I do hope you're not abusing Mr Charles's hospitality by upsetting his guests. Why . . .' He patted Michael's shoulder affectionately. 'Poor Michael's gone quite pale; almost, wouldn't you say my dear,' he turned to his bride, 'as if he was exsanguinated?'

The bride's lips twitched even more. 'Not quite,' she said examining Michael with an expert eye.

The sergeant clenched his fists and his jocular tone was a little forced. 'There's no need for legal advice this time,' he said. 'The case is closed.'

'And the culprit?' said Kalazian. 'Safely behind bars?'

'Not exactly,' said the sergeant and the twinkle returned to his eyes. 'I don't think they bother with bars any more at the loony bin.'

'Mad,' said Kalazian.

'Stark raving,' said the sergeant. 'A history as long as your arm.'

Though the hospital he had been in was a different place entirely, Michael could see the night nurse at the end of the dormitory, the torch in her hand shining on the face of his young Maori friend.

'He did it for me,' he said.

'That's right,' said the sergeant, 'but like I say, he's mad.'

Mad or not, and in spite of the fact that he'd given him seven dollars, Michael felt a perverse gratitude. He wanted to thank the Maori for his time and trouble, for his honesty and integrity. His friend could have taken the money, spent it on another Uncle's hamburger and chips, which is probably what he did do, and left it at that. Instead, he was as good as his word, or almost. He hadn't killed the four hoons but he'd tried. That was the important thing; and what's more he'd done it with little regard for his own comfort and safety. Michael thought it would be a good idea, when things settled down, to visit his friend and maybe take him a carton of cigarettes. There'd probably be a lot of idle time in the loony bin with not much else to do but smoke. Smoking of course was strictly forbidden in the hospital he had been in; not that that stopped some of the more determined ones. In fact, when he thought of it there were a lot of determined ones. Most of his fellow patients smoked when the nurses' backs were turned, or even in some cases when they weren't.

'No,' the sergeant was explaining to Kalazian between bites of whitebait fritter. 'No need for bush lawyers this time. The case is closed.' He wiped his fingers on the lapel of his jacket. 'Anyway, I've bigger fish to fry.'

'On the trail of Mr Big, are we?' Kalazian was obviously stung at being referred to as a bush lawyer. His bride wet her lips and snuggled closer to his ear.

'Someone,' said the sergeant, 'who likes to think he is.'

Kalazian's bride opened her lips and licked her pearly white teeth. In the time it took the sergeant to empty his glass her black varnished fingernails grew longer and sharper. If Kalazian had given the word Michael knew she would have had the sergeant's throat out before he'd taken the glass from his lips. Fortunately or not, Kalazian didn't give the word. His attention along with everyone else's was distracted by the further dimming of the already dim lights, followed by a drum roll topped off with a threatening cymbal. No one dared move.

The spotlight lit up Mr Charles's over-rouged face. He was dressed in an evening suit and his hair was Brylcreemed and parted down the middle. He had a hand microphone but it was only a prop; everyone could hear his unamplified voice.

'Ladeez and gentlemen,' he said.

'Not many of those here,' someone called.

There was laughter but Mr Charles, undeterred, continued,

'Meine Damen und Herren, mesdames et messieurs, guten Abend, bon soir, hello, good evening and welcome.' He took a bow.

'Piss off,' said the heckler and got another laugh.

Mr Charles stood up straight, adjusted his bow tie, gave the ends of his parted-down-the-middle hair a flick and looking down his nose at the heckler said, 'I can see there's an element here tonight.' He held up his white-gloved hand to acknowledge and quell the laughter.

'You've had the unofficial entertainment,' he confirmed and the spotlight picked out Calpurnia, a white carnation attached to the shoulder of his shapeless green frock. 'A big hand for Calpurnia,' but the applause had already begun. Calpurnia bowed his head and sheepishly shuffled his feet. The spotlight swung back to Mr Charles and Calpurnia's applause died away. He opened his mouth to speak but before he could say anything there was the roll of the drum topped off with a threatening cymbal. It got a laugh as it was supposed to, but Mr Charles feigned annoyance and glared at the drummer.

'Thank you,' he said with his teeth tightly shut then smiled at the audience to show all was forgiven.

'Now,' he said, 'for the official entertainment.'

Kalazian, with his free elbow, nudged Michael. 'This should be good. Mr Charles's friends are very talented.'

Mr Charles spread his hands wide, turned sideways and backed away from the spotlight. The ever-popular Marlene Dietrich, in top hat and tights, sang with her cruel mouth and S.S. sneer, 'I Can't Give You Anything But Love'. She was very good and Michael said so as he applauded her. The sergeant thought so too. 'You know,' he said, 'I always thought the real Marlene Dietrich was a bloke.'

Michael noticed that Kalazian wasn't clapping. He had his hand down the unzipped front of his bride's leather skirt and was searching around as if he'd lost a fifty-cent piece. Mrs Kalazian would be in her spotless front room with the curtains drawn, the lights out and a bottle of sherry and a glass close by.

Liza Minelli was next; Sally Bowles in a bowler hat and

mascara-clogged eyes. She sang 'Cabaret' and on the last note kicked her leg and sent one of her high-heel shoes into the audience. A young man with technicolor blue-black hair caught it and hugged it to his chest. Liza with black streams running down her cheeks hobbled across to him, snatched the shoe from his grasp and limped into the bedroom followed by hoots and jeers.

'Oh,' Mr Charles exclaimed with his hand to his heart and a look of deep pain on his face, 'the agonies of stardom.'

The sergeant laughed like a friendly local copper while Kalazian gave up his futile search and applauded too. 'Encore, encore,' he called but as his bride subsided beside him his calls were drowned out by a row of menacing young thugs hired for the occasion.

'We want a melodrama,' they chanted, stomping their feet and clapping. Mr Charles stopped them with a stern look and a wink. He pointed to the heavens and in an incongruously deep and commanding voice for a man of his persuasions, said, 'A melodrama you shall have,' and brought his hand down. The spotlight went out. The room went black. There were whisperings and scamperings and one or two nervous giggles. There was strange music, as if people not right in the head were playing flutes and violins softly in the room next door.

The scene was a shabby bedroom. A pale blue light came through the window. There was an unmade bed, clothes hanging dead over the back of a chair and a woman with lines at the corners of her mouth and eyes sitting on the end of the bed with her back to the audience. The strange music tailed off and a mournful voice called outside the window, *Flores, flores, flores por los meurtes.* Kalazian, breathing his brandy-flavoured breath into Michael's ear, snorted quietly.

The woman shuddered as the voice drifted off into the distance. There was a gentle knock at her door which rustled the thin paper coverings of the wall. With a sharp intake of breath the woman darted her head towards the door. Her hand clutched at the collar of her dressing gown and her body stiffened. The knock came again, still gentle but more insistent.

She arose with a sigh and opened the door. A black-haired, black-moustachioed man in a long black overcoat entered the room, his eyes blazing melodramatically. Without thinking, Michael made a sudden move forward but Kalazian caught his arm.

'Calm yourself,' he whispered. 'It's only a play.'

On reflection, Michael could see that it was. The black-haired man wasn't Mallis; he was one of Mr Charles's talented friends. And the woman wasn't Anna, though in the pale blue light and the shadows and the imagination it was hard to tell. The man took the woman in his arms and without a word kissed her violently. She swooned and there was a murmur and ripple of applause. He lifted the woman's limp body in his arms and took her to the bed, laid her carefully in the middle, smoothed her hair away from her face and took four large white handkerchiefs from his pocket, flicking each one in turn. Michael was relieved. The play was turning into a good old-fashioned magic act. The stage would soon be full of doves but the black-haired man used the handkerchiefs to tie the woman's hands and feet to the corners of the bed.

The woman awoke and tried to pull herself free but her struggles were in vain. The man lit a long cigarette and for tradition's sake and the delight of the audience twirled the end of his moustache. In the pale blue light the tip of his cigarette glowed red. He roughly pulled the dressing gown away from the woman's shoulder and held the cigarette above her. The curtain fell; there was a stifled scream. Someone in the audience started to clap but no one joined in. The clapping stopped and there was a muffled cough as the strange music wafted through the walls from the room next door. The curtains opened again.

At one end of the stage was a dark and gloomy forest full of plywood trees and crêpe paper creepers. At the other end was a clearing with a cheery little gingerbread cottage painted on the canvas backdrop and slightly creased in the middle. Manfully forcing his way through the tangle of the gloomy forest was a handsome young prince in white tights, tunic and feathered hat. A sigh went up from the audience as he stepped into the light of the clearing and stood resolutely before the gingerbread cottage.

'What oh,' he called in a manly voice.

A merry old woodcutter appeared, stuffed full of pillows and wrapped in a moth-eaten pullover. With his cap in his hand he tugged his forelock.

'Ah . . . your eminence, your prominence, your bright luminescence,' he said and bowed in obsequious awe. The handsome prince took it all in his stride. 'I am a seeker of wisdom, knowledge and truth,' he announced with a flourish.

'Indeed you are sir, indeed you are,' said the woodcutter, bobbing and bowing so much one of his pillows slipped out from under his pullover. He stuffed it back and said, 'But you'll have time while you're searching to rescue a beautiful princess?'

'Why,' said the prince suddenly frowning, 'have you got one?'

'Indeed we have, sir.' The merry woodcutter shuffled closer to the handsome prince. 'Indeed we have.' He looked over both his shoulders and carefully around both sides of the prince then beckoned him even closer and in a stage whisper said, 'In yonder castle.' He pointed offstage above the heads of the audience.

Michael was tempted to turn round and look but with an effort kept his eyes on the stage. Several members of the audience, less able to resist temptation, turned their heads and giggled. The woodcutter, in superstitious fear, shielded his eyes, turned his face from the castle and quickly crossed himself.

'The Dark Lord,' he said, 'keeps her there for his private pleasure.'

The handsome prince with a look of stern forbearance put his hand on the hilt of his sword and said, 'How dreadful.'

The woodcutter shook his head. 'It is that, your eminence, it is that,' and drawing the prince even closer said, 'On a still day like today, if you listen very carefully, you can hear her torments.' He put a finger to his lips. Everything went quiet. The woodcutter, the prince, Michael and all the audience held their breaths.

From a long way off came a thin high scream, so far and faint it might not have been real. The prince drew his sparkly silver painted sword and shook it in the direction of the castle. 'I,' he said, his noble brow and handsome features burning with indignation, 'will fight and destroy the Dark Lord.'

When the cheer from the audience died down a strange transformation came over the woodcutter. He drew his pullover over his head and the pillows fell to the floor. He wore a long black robe spattered with crescent moons, ringed planets and sheriff-badge stars. From behind his back he took a pointed black hat patterned in the same fashion and placed it magnificently on his head.

'Put up thy sword,' he ordered. 'The Dark Lord will not be destroyed that way or any other way. He can never be destroyed.'

The prince did as commanded and sulkily asked, 'Why not?'

'It's a mystery to me,' said the wizard, 'but there you are.' He shrugged. 'We're stuck with it.'

Lulled by the magic, Michael hardly noticed the sergeant jotting down notes in a mean little notebook, or Kalazian scratching his belly through a hole in his moth-eaten pullover.

'But I must save the princess,' said the handsome prince without the slightest sign of a wrinkle in his tights.

'It can be done,' said the wizard, 'but it will take courage.'

'I've got that,' said the prince.

'And fortitude,' said the wizard.

'That too.'

'And boldness.'

'Naturally.'

'And resolve,' said the wizard counting each point on his fingers.

'Obviously,' said the prince with his hands on his hips.

'And tenacity.'

'I,' shouted the prince, 'have all these qualities and more in abundance.'

'And magic?'

The prince faltered. He took his hands from his hips and tapped the tip of his noble chin. 'Ah well,' he said. 'I haven't any of that, I'm afraid. I don't suppose you could let me borrow some?'

'Borrow,' said the wizard and steadied his pointed hat. 'I have magic and more in abundance. You can have as much as you like.' He plunged his hand deep inside the pocket of his robe, brought out a small bottle and held it up for all to see. It contained, as all such bottles should, a suspicious green liquid.

'Two drops of this,' said the wizard, 'and the beautiful princess will be free of the Dark Lord forever.'

The sergeant flipped over a page in his notebook and scribbled vigorously.

'I'd do it myself,' the wizard said, 'but I haven't the courage, the fortitude, the boldness etcetera, etcetera, etcetera.'

'I,' shouted the prince again, 'have all these qualities and more in abundance. Give me the magic bottle that I might save the princess.'

As the Wizard handed the bottle over, the curtain fell, and the strange music crept in from the room next door. 'It's poison,' the audience hissed and the back of Michael's neck tightened and went cold. The sergeant still scribbling in the notebook muttered, 'There's murder afoot here. I can smell it.'

When the curtains opened again, save for some lumpy brown sacks scattered across the floor the stage was bare and lit by a dim and dusty twilight. For a minute or longer nothing happened then, one by one, the sacks began to move. There were people inside them, mumbling and coughing and crawling about, bumping into each other, shouting and growling and grabbing blindly. Suddenly the spotlight lit up a figure at one end of the stage. It was the prince, though not so handsome now, his feather bent, his tunic torn and grimy, his tights wrinkled and twisted. His face was a ghastly white with painted black eyes sloping down at the sides and a painted black mouth to match. A groan went up from the audience.

On either side of the shattered prince and just visible outside the spotlight were the wizard and a plain-clothes policeman with a bristly moustache. The policeman picked up a sack and opened it at the top. With the help of the wizard the prince climbed into the sack and curled up inside. The policeman tied a rope tightly around the top; the wizard looked at him and they both shook their heads slowly. Between them they carried the sack to the centre of the stage, dropped it among all the other sacks and made their exits with heads bowed. When Michael looked back at the centre stage and all the mumbling, growling, crawling sacks, he wasn't sure which one contained the prince.

The curtain fell; the lights went up. There was cheering, whistling and clapping. The play was an enormous success. Mr Charles wandered amongst his guests accepting with unfeigned pride and pleasure their congratulations. Each person he spoke to called him 'darling,' took his head in their hands and kissed him loudly on each cheek. 'Divine,' they said, 'simply divine.'

It was 'a stunning performance', 'an intellectual *tour de force*', 'a biting satire', 'a symbolic representation of our doomed society', 'a passionate portrayal of the barbarity lurking beneath the thin veneer of civilisation'. One of the uncouth louts who had demanded a melodrama, mumbling through a mouthful of half-chewed potato chips said, 'It was good but I wanted a stabbing.'

'And,' said Mr Charles daintily pecking him on the forehead, 'you'll get one if you're not careful, you uncouth lout.' The lout roared with laughter and sprayed everyone around him with chips.

Mr Charles brushed the debris from his hair and eyebrows and made his way to Kalazian, whose bride had now deserted him. 'What did you think?' he asked eagerly.

'I preferred the part where I had my hand down the front of your niece's skirt,' Kalazian said.

Mr Charles covered his mouth to stifle his shocked laughter. 'You wicked old roué.' He gave Kalazian a push. Kalazian staggered playfully off balance but righted himself in time to catch the claret in his glass before it slopped over.

'Michael,' said Mr Charles, turning to him. 'What did *you* think?' He lowered his voice. 'You know the play was mainly for you.'

'I'm not sure,' said Michael. He felt as if his thoughts had been stuffed into a sack and the top tied so they couldn't get out. Kalazian placed an avuncular, carbuncular arm around his shoulder and told him not to worry. 'It's only a play.'

From nowhere, or perhaps from under the carpet, came the young man with the wispy beard and glasses like milk bottle bottoms. 'But surely,' he said, 'to dismiss the play as merely a play is to deny the fact that it presents us with an aspect of reality which, because it is concentrated and stylised, is more real than the reality of everyday life which, in many ways, is largely illusion?' He waited breathlessly for Kalazian's response.

Kalazian wrinkled his nose at him and looked him up and down. 'Flypaper,' he said.

The earnest young man's glasses slipped down his nose. He pushed them back with a tremulous finger. 'Flypaper,' he repeated and drifted back into the crowd, nodding thoughtfully.

Michael giggled but Kalazian stroked the back of his head to stop him. 'Oh dear,' said Mr Charles, stamping his foot petulantly. 'When you don't want one they're everywhere and when you do want one they're nowhere.'

'What's that?' asked Kalazian.

'Why, a policeman,' said Mr Charles and sure enough the sergeant had gone.

10

Michael had never had consumption. His disease or condition, whatever it was, was certainly full of shadows but not the ones that show up on X-ray. There were a number of possibilities, none of them true. The current one was that it was a defect of memory. In this theory a person's memory is interfered with in some as-yet inexplicable way. The effect of this interference is to take away memories of things that happened, which is not at all unusual, and insert memories of things that didn't happen, which is very unusual. For example, a person might put a pair of purple socks in the top drawer of his bedside locker and the next morning remember distinctly that he had put them in the bottom drawer. He has therefore forgotten something which did happen and remembered something which did not. He is surprised and perhaps a little angry to discover that his socks are missing. He is surprised, confused and perhaps a little frightened when he finally finds his socks in the top drawer. Of course the person experiencing this trick of memory soon recognises it for the trick it is and might, in fact probably will, laugh it off as a vaguely annoying but essentially innocuous event. Events like these, he will tell himself, are very common and by the end of the day, such is the kindness of memory, he will have forgotten all about it. But as a pimple on the end of the nose is to a full raging case of haemorrhagic smallpox, so is this minor defect of memory to the awful destruction unleashed in Michael's case.

'Somewhat floridly expressed,' Kalazian said when he came calling, 'but an interesting theory nonetheless.'

In spite of the fact that he was sorry he hadn't succeeded in murdering Kalazian, Michael still valued his judgment and looked forward to every second Friday when he visited him.

'It certainly explains a lot of your behaviour,' said Kalazian as he paced slowly with Michael past the phoenix palms and the lopped-off plane trees alongside the hospital chapel.

It explained for example how, some days after Mr Charles's party, the sergeant had thanked Michael for having been so co-operative in providing a full written confession of his crimes when Michael couldn't remember providing it. It also explained why Michael couldn't remember writing the written confession especially as it was written in what he took to be Kalazian's copperplate hand but which was in fact his own copperplate hand. Kalazian's writing, which Kalazian had demonstrated for Michael and the sergeant's benefit, was a barely legible scrawl.

'The result,' Kalazian said, 'of overuse of the ballpoint pen.'

According to Michael's theory, these unusual occurrences are explained simply as examples of forgetting that which has happened. The second, and more bizarre part of his theory — that of remembering things which never happened — explained, if not quite so simply, the even more strange and frightening aspects of his case. It explained for example why, with their helmets still on their heads and their regulation issue black gumboots covered in clay, six policemen, after digging holes all over Kalazian's back garden, had not unearthed a single body. Later, in the interrogation room at Auckland Central the sergeant had placed a telephone directory on Michael's abdomen and, in his frustrated search for the truth, punched it as hard as he could.

'No bruises,' he explained.

Michael, with tears in his eyes, wanted to thank the sergeant and help him in his search but at that time he hadn't formulated his theory and besides, when he opened his mouth to speak, nothing came out. The sergeant obligingly hit him again.

Perhaps out of a sense of guilt, but Michael hoped more from friendship and compassion, the sergeant visited Michael every other Tuesday. Michael looked forward to these visits almost as much as he looked forward to Kalazian's.

'How's Mrs Kalazian?' Michael politely enquired, not being able to remember whether he had already asked the question.

'She's had the landscape gardeners in,' said Kalazian and sat down on a bench outside the chapel to catch his breath. 'Didn't I tell you?'

'I can't remember,' said Michael, sitting down beside him.

'No, of course not,' Kalazian chuckled. 'The mess your local friendly coppers made of the back garden prompted her. She's been wanting to do it for years.'

Kalazian took out a large white monogrammed handkerchief and wiped his brow. 'You wouldn't recognise the place now,' he said. 'There's a paved barbecue area, ponga logs, a rockery. It's a great comfort to her after all she's been through.'

'Has she forgiven me?' asked Michael.

Kalazian, as avuncular as ever, patted Michael's knee.

'Michael,' he said. 'Mrs Kalazian has never blamed you or condemned you. She loves you still, as I do.'

'Then,' said Michael, 'she might come here one day with you.'

'Ah.' Kalazian replaced his handkerchief in his top pocket. 'I see,' he slowly shook his head. 'It's you who must forgive her,

I'm afraid. She tries to come but fear of places like this is too much for her.'

Michael groaned. He was so acutely sensitive that he could develop the peculiar malady that afflicted him but not so sensitive to the maladies of others. 'I'm sorry,' he said quickly. 'I forgot.'

Kalazian tutted and sighed. 'Michael,' he said gently, 'Mrs Kalazian's family, apart from an elder sister killed in a motorcycle accident, are all horribly alive and living, thank God, in Dunedin. Mrs Kalazian just doesn't like these places.'

'And Anna left without paying the rent, and Mallis has returned to his wife and children,' said Michael. 'The trouble is,' he gave a short laugh, 'I can't believe a word you tell me.'

'Very wise,' said Kalazian and waved to Michael's young Maori friend walking past with a half-eaten hamburger in his hand. The tip of Kalazian's little finger had a white scar just below the fingerprint which reminded Michael. The night of Mr Charles's party, after the play was over, the hired young louts had called out in chorus, 'Author, author,' and stamped their feet. The spotlight hovered over Mr Charles but eventually settled on Kalazian who, with all the modesty of a corrupt and corpulent Byzantine emperor, gave a drunken wave, fell forward and spilt his claret on Mr Charles's carpet.

The play had unhinged Michael to the point where he saw everything so clearly his eyes nearly burst. In less than a second everything was explained. Kalazian was evil, pure evil. He revelled in confusion, distortion, destruction and lies. When he helped Kalazian to his feet and wiped the claret from his chin and moth-eaten pullover, assurances that it was only a play didn't fool Michael one bit. Kalazian dug his chin into his chest and belched but it did him no good. Enveloped in a miasma of garlic, brandy, claret, smoked eel and peppercorn salami, Michael wasn't to be put off. He could see from the look in Kalazian's eye that he knew the truth was out. Kalazian felt for Michael's hand and took it in both of his. Steadying himself he said. 'What's done is done, Michael. It would have turned out this way no matter what. Try not to think ill of me.'

Out of memory of their friendship Michael tried to do as he was asked but it didn't work. The ill that he felt was strong enough and lasted long enough to result in Kalazian temporarily losing the tip of his little finger. After all the business with the play and the police and the holes in the garden, confessions and telephone books, in an attack reminiscent of Mallis's attempts on Michael's life, Michael, with a kitchen knife borrowed from Mrs Kalazian, attempted to stab Kalazian through the heart. Like the instrument of God's justice on earth his arm rose but before it fell Kalazian, quick as a cockroach, scurried under the kitchen table and, worse still, put doubt in Michael's way.

'Michael,' he called and banged his head on the underside of the table. A buttered scone jumped off a side plate and landed on the tabletop buttered side down. 'I'm not the Dark Lord. I'm only a man in a moth-eaten pullover.'

Already rattled by the fate of the scone and without looking what he was doing, Michael threw the knife to the floor where it caught the tip of Kalazian's outstretched little finger and sliced it off. Mrs Kalazian stitched it back on with a needle and thread while Kalazian and Michael drank half a bottle of Coruba rum between them to deaden the pain.

Kalazian was waving to the chaplain nervously checking through the door of his chapel to see who was talking. When the door closed he kept his little finger wagging and grinned at Michael.

'Pure evil,' he said and laughed.

Michael tried to look shamefaced and laughed with him but he still wasn't sure.

'You're still not sure, are you?' said Kalazian and stopped laughing.

'The pills they give you here,' said Michael lowering his voice, 'take away certainty.'

Kalazian lowered his voice too. 'You could always spit them down the toilet.'

'Doubt is encouraged here,' said Michael. 'The last time I was certain, I almost killed you.'

Kalazian unwrapped the silver paper on a tube of individually wrapped butterscotch lollies, unwrapped an individual wrapping and popped a butterscotch into his mouth. 'I'm sure the people here have what they believe to be your best interests at heart.'

'I suppose they do,' said Michael, but wasn't so sure.

'And yet,' went on Kalazian between sucks of his butterscotch, 'it saddens me to see a seeker of wisdom and truth content to live in doubt.'

'I'm not content,' said Michael. 'If I was I'd pick up one of the stick-on smiles they dish out here and put my name down for a good citizen award.' He realised he'd raised his voice and quickly put his head down, hoping no one had noticed.

Kalazian offered him a butterscotch but Michael shook his head. 'What's the matter?' asked Kalazian, trying to keep his laughter back, 'Don't you trust me?'

'No,' said Michael. He took the individually wrapped butterscotch lolly, unwrapped the individual wrapping and popped the lolly into his mouth.

'That's the spirit,' said Kalazian and Michael marvelled at the man's ability to inspire him. 'Down the toilet with the pills. Down the toilet with them all. And the next time I come calling I expect you to try to kill me.'

PACIFIC WRITERS SERIES

The book you have been reading is part of Reed's Pacific Writers Series, a show-case for the finest fiction from New Zealand and the Pacific Islands. Other titles available in the series are listed below, but for further information please write to Pacific Writers Series, Reed Books, Private Bag Birkenhead, Auckland 10, New Zealand.

Other titles in the Pacific Writers Series:

Tangi	Witi Ihimaera
The Frigate Bird	Alistair Campbell
Visitors	John Cranna
Earthly Delights	Nick Hyde
The New Land	Bill Manhire
Pet Shop	Ian Middleton
The Veteran Perils	Damien Wilkins
Nights with Grace	Rosie Scott
Blessed Art Thou Among Women	Christine Johnston
Maori Girl	Noel Hilliard
Sidewinder	Alistair Campbell (October 1991)